CHURCH IN THE WOODS

by Linda MorningStar

PUBLISH AMERICA

PublishAmerica
Baltimore

First printing

All characters in this book are fictitious, and any resemblance to real persons, living or dead, is coincidental.

PublishAmerica has allowed this work to remain exactly as the author intended, verbatim, without editorial input.

ISBN: 978-1-4489-8544-9
PUBLISHED BY PUBLISHAMERICA, LLLP
www.publishamerica.com
Baltimore

Printed in the United States of America

This book is dedicated to

Melissa
who as a young girl
planted a seed
in my heart
to write this story

and to

Dancing Turtle
who opened my heart
with his love and
who now resides in
the spirit world
patiently awaiting
my arrival

Thank you to

Linda
my spirit sister
who by her faith
encourages
and strengthens
me daily

Chapter One

Heaving a sigh, I plop my elbow on the dining room table, lean my head on my hand and stare reluctantly at the bowl of cereal in front of me. I hate raisins. My mother, (who loves them), insists on buying cereal with raisins because, "They're good for you."

Actually, they do slow down my eating. I suppose that is good for me. I begin the morning ritual of picking raisins out of the cereal and stacking them neatly on the napkin next to me. I wonder how high I can build a raisin pyramid.

"Stanley has the nicest kitchen," Mother says. "It's so much newer than ours."

I could care less. I stare at her back as she leans over the kitchen sink and runs a sponge around the rim of it. Mother is forever cleaning.

The worst part is, the more she cleans the more she chatters. As usual, this morning is no exception. And, as usual, I wish she would shut up. I am sick of hearing about her new boyfriend, Stanley Hood. I wish he would go on one of those trips he is always bragging about and never come back.

Listening to Mother ramble on can drive me crazy. My dad used to say, "It's just Mother's way to flitter around and chirp like a bird,"—but then, he was always making excuses for her. It occurs to me my mother is more like a chicken running around with its head cut off, except of course, for the talking. Anyway, it's not as though she actually talks to me. It's more that she talks at me. As long as I nod my head or grunt "un huh" once in a while, she seems satisfied. I'm pretty sure my dad felt the same way, except he'd pretend it didn't bother him.

I place the last raisin on top of the pyramid, wad up the napkin, and crunch on cereal while Mother describes in elaborate detail how beautiful Stanley's condo is. She is starting to get on my nerves. I glance at the rooster clock. The morning is slipping away. Thank goodness! Stanley should show up soon and whisk her off some where. Then I can snuggle up in my dad's old flannel shirt and sleep the day away.

I grab the remote control and click on the TV to drown out Mother's voice. There is nothing on but stupid Sunday morning stuff. I flip it back off the very second the phone rings.

"I'll get it." I stretch across the table and reach for the phone. "No, I'm not going today, next week, or the week after," I state flatly into the receiver. "When are you going to quit asking?"

"Never," came a cheerful response. "You mean too much to me. And, by the way, Chickadee, you should at least say hello when you pick up the phone, you never know who might be calling. What if it was Harold?"

I wish it was. Unfortunately, Harold Barnes—the cutest boy in the whole school—doesn't seem to know I exist. I ignore the Harold comment and get right to the heart of the matter.

"It's always you at quarter of eleven on Sunday morning, Marcy. And, truthfully, I'm getting tired of it. We have this stupid conversation every week." I don't even try to keep the irritation out of my voice.

"Then why don't you come back to church with me," she pleads. "Then we could stop talking about it. Besides, it would help you."

"Sure," I say with sarcasm, "like it helped my dad. No thanks."

"Oh Chickadee, I wish you could stop being angry at God. He didn't cause the accident—it just happened. Mom and I are still praying for you. We pray every day for God to open your heart to Him."

"Well, you can just stop it. You should support my feelings instead of pray for me. After all, Marcy you are supposed to be my best friend."

"I am your best—." I hear her say as I slam the phone down. Obviously, Marcy doesn't know what it's like to lose a dad because she never had one. But I don't see how can she think God's not responsible for my dad's death. Only God could make the March wind blow hard enough to break a tree limb and send it crashing through the windshield of my dad's car the moment he drives by.

And where was Jesus? Isn't he suppose to be the healer? My dad loved Jesus and trusted Him and for what? Jesus didn't even try to help.

"Is Marcy still trying to get you to go to church?" Mother asks, attacking the sink full force.

"I tried to tell your father, years ago, not to get mixed up in church," she went on to say. "I told him all that God-stuff was nonsense, but he wouldn't listen. He never should have gotten you involved. Now Stanley, never goes to church. He says he has better things to do with his time and money."

"Un huh," I say, and wonder why God didn't kill Stanley and leave my dad alone.

I turn and gaze out the window at the new blanket of snow on the ground. It's a beautiful January day. The sky is filled with patches of blue and the sun sparkles on the clean fallen snow causing the earth to look fresh and new, and pure. I can't help but smile as a gust of wind swirls around the corner of the barn and casts a thousand tiny diamonds in its wake.

Suddenly I long to be in the midst of it and wish Marcy would skip church so we could ride our snowmobiles together—fat chance of that happening. I'm beginning to feel sorry I hung up on her. I do miss going to church with her and I miss all the fun we use to have together. We were inseparable. I especially miss the overnight stays and fireside chats with her mom. We use to laugh so much. But since my dad died—except for school—we hardly see each other. I shake my head. Every day is such a drag any more. I can't wait until Mother leaves so I can go back to bed. Maybe I'll get lucky and dream about my dad.

"Chickadee Marie Bird, are you listening to me?"

Startled, I turn and look at Mother. She is leaning against the counter with her hands on her hips—looking straight at me.

"I heard you," I exaggerate the words. "Stanley has a lovely home in the new housing development on the edge of town, lots of money, and a great job." I lift my spoon to take the last bite of cereal.

"And," she says, drawing the word out, "I said I'm going to marry him."

Chapter Two

Marry him? Mother's words are like an electric shock to my brain. The spoon falls from my hand, hits the edge of the table, and bounces to the floor splattering milk and cereal along the way. I ignore the mess and search my mothers' face for a sign she might be joking. But Mother does not joke. The cereal in my stomach slowly turns to lead. I try to stand. My legs feel like rubber and I fall back into the seat.

"You—you've got to be kidding," I stammer. "You—you hardly know him."

"I know him well enough," Mother says with a huff and turns back to the sink. She always turns her back to me when she's annoyed. I stare at her dumbfounded. She slides the row of bluebird canisters toward her and wipes the counter behind them as through everything was normal.

"Stanley is a wonderful man," she adds matter-of-fact, "and we are going to be married. Don't think I haven't noticed how unfriendly you are toward him and I want that to change. It's time you started showing him a little respect."

Respect? How can I respect some jerk who always calls me "Little Chickadee-dee-dee"?—I scream inside my head with clenched teeth. It is all I can do not to let it out—but I know better. To disagree with mother on anything always makes the situation worse.

I wish my dad was here—he would know what to say. At the first sign of a problem with Mother he'd whisk me off to another room and talk with me, and then he would go talk to her and smooth things over. But he's gone, and now I have to deal with her on my own. It's not fair. I watch her wipe off the bird canisters one by one and push them back against the wall. I don't know what to do.

"And another thing," Mother says, "It's time to get rid of all these birds." She waves her hand around the room. "I'm planning a yard sale in the Spring to sell everything. I want to make a brand new start. Besides all these birds mean nothing to Stanley."

My mouth drops open as I look at the collection of porcelain birds on the windowsill, the cardinal salt and pepper shakers on the stove and the china cabinet next to me brimming with different kinds of ceramic birds. I see the mass of tiny bird magnets covering the refrigerator.

I think of all the chickadees lining the shelves in my bedroom and of the special chickadee Christmas ornaments stored away in the closet. I always look forward to Christmas Eve when I carefully unpack them and hang them on the tree. Each year my dad would hand me a new chickadee ornament, and I would put that on the tree, too, next to the others. I have thirteen—one for every year of my life—except this year.

Every Christmas Eve, without fail, dad would tell me the same story.

"When I met your mother," he would say, "It was love at first sight, and when I learned her name was Robin Crane, I knew she was the one for me. I told her my name was Jay Bird and she thought I was making fun of her name." Then he would laugh and say, "I told her right off that two birds were better than one and we should get married. Before long, I bought her an engagement ring with two doves and a diamond in the middle. After that, we went crazy buying each other bird gifts."

Then he would say, "Now, the very moment your mother told me we were going to have a baby, a little chickadee landed right on the windowsill. We decided then and there you would be a girl, and we would name you Chickadee. When you popped out all scrawny with fluffy hair sticking out all over, we knew it was meant to be." That's when he would reach over and ruffle my hair.

Tears gather in the corner of my eyes. Getting rid of the birds would be like getting rid of the best part of me. My chest tightens. I feel as though I am going to suffocate.

"You,—you can't get rid of the birds," I manage to squeak.

"Of course I can," my mother says, apparently not noticing my discomfort.

"After Stanley and I get married we will live with him."

Live with Stanley? I struggle desparately not to cry in front Mother, but I can't bear the thought of it. The tears pour down my face.

"Mother—please," I sob, "What—what about our house? What about me?".

"Oh Chickadee, stop crying. You're being rediculous. Of course you'll go with me. The only reason we moved to this old farmhouse in the first place is because your grandfather—that crazy old Indian—left it to your father and he was too sentimental to sell it. But he's gone now, and I don't have to live here any longer. Life goes on and I mean to go with it. Stanley is what I need."

"Don't call my grandfather a crazy old Indian. He was Native American and Dad said he was Ojibwa and a good man—and I never even got to meet him." The words burst forth before I can stop them, but I guess it doesn't matter now—when Mother gets done there won't be any trace of my dad left. The situation can't get any worse. "And now Dad's dead too," I say, getting louder. "He hasn't even been dead a year and you're trying to erase him off the face of the earth."

Mother turns and glares at me, but I don't care.

"How can you throw everything out and start over with some

horrible jerk you hardly know?" I practically scream at her.
"That's enough!" Mother's voice is cold and hard. "You will not raise your voice to me again—ever! And you are not to call Stanley names. I will decide what is best and you will do what I say." Something inside me snaps. I feel like I am seeing my mother for the first time. I understand now what my dad spent his whole life shielding me from. A strange calmness comes over me. I slowly stand and wipe away the tears.

"No, I won't," I say with certainty. "Not any more. You don't care about what is best for me—you have never even considered it—not once in my whole life. You never loved me or Dad. All you care about is you."

An odd look comes over Mother's face. I can't stand to be around her a second longer. I dash to the backroom and snatch my snowmobile suit off the hook. I notice I still have my pajamas on, but I don't care. I have to get out of here. Now!

Chapter Three

With one quick thrust, I squeeze the throttle. The snowmobile lunges ahead with a roar, knocking me off balance. I grip the handle bars and fight to pull myself forward. The right ski skims up over the edge of a snow-hidden stone bordering the flower bed. The sudden shift of the snowmobile jolts me back in the seat. I grasp the sides of the machine with my knees and lean into the race position my dad taught me long ago.

"Come back here!" I hear Mother shriek over the roar of the snowmobile.

No way! Without a backward glance, I speed away from the house. I bound across the yard, through the fence opening, and into the meadow. Flying over a snowdrift, the snowmobile hits the ground with a thud. My face shield jars loose from the helmet and falls forward. I want to push it back so I can feel the cold sting of air on my cheeks, but refuse to let go of the handle bars. I push the throttle harder. Blood pumps through my veins—faster and faster—with the increasing speed of the machine. I wonder which will explode first—the snowmobile or me. Would it really matter? Who would care?

Reaching the base of the hill, I fishtail around a clump of evergreens and clip a snow-covered branch with my shoulder. Snow swirls about and sticks to my face shield. I press on, upward, barely able to see the twisting turns as I wind my way through the stretch of woods connecting to the old trail road along Cemetery Ridge.

One quick turn and I barrel down the narrow trail past the old abandoned cemetery. I come to a wide spot in the trail and see tracks where snowmobiles have turned around but I am not ready to go back. I press on through the heavy snow making a new path as I go deeper into the woods.

Suddenly, the snowmobile seems to hesitate and I push the throttle harder. The motor spits and sputters and comes to an abrupt halt. Instant silence surrounds me. With it, a knowing fear grips my heart. Frantically, I try to start the snowmobile, but the motor will not turn over.

"Chickadee," my dad use to say in his most serious voice, "There are two rules you must follow. You must never—never snowmobile alone and you must always check the gas tank before you leave the yard. You know how unpredictable these Wisconsin winters can be. A person stranded out in the cold could freeze to death."

"Oh Dad, I'm sorry," I mutter as tears fill my eyes. I slide back in the seat, pull off my helmet, and wipe my eyes with the back of my glove.

Stepping off the snowmobile, I sink into the snow. Something about sinking into that snow makes me angry.

"You know what, Dad?" I say louder, "I change my mind. I am not sorry! Not one bit!"

I throw my helmet down and kick the snowmobile as hard as I can. Pain shoots through my ankle.

"It's all your fault, anyway! If you hadn't died, Mother would never have met that jerk Stanley Hood and I wouldn't be in this mess. How could you leave me?" I scream at the top of my lungs.

"I hate this! I hate this!" I fling myself in the snow and pound it to the ground. I keep screaming and crying, and pounding until I collapse.

Exhausted, I roll over on my back and stare at the sky. I inhale deep breaths of the frosty air as I watch the clouds overtake the sun and turn the day a dull gray. The wind blows across my face and a chill runs through me. I force myself up, lean against the snowmobile, and brush off the snow. I look around. I see only one choice in front of me—walk.

Taking off my gloves, I fumble through my pockets for a tissue and blow my nose. The wind picks up and blows hard against my back. I remember hearing the temperature may plunge below zero by evening. If only I had taken time to put warm clothes on under my snowmobile suit. I shake the snow out of my helmet and wipe off the face shield: wearing it will at least keep the wind out of my face. I wish I had grabbed a scarf. Heck, I wish lots of things, but it doesn't make any difference now.

The only place for me to go is to Marcy's. I wonder what she will say when she sees me wearing my pajamas. I stuff my hands back in my gloves and start trudging through the snow.

With each step, my ankle reminds me how hard I kicked the snowmobile. I pull a broken branch from a tree limb and use it for a crutch. It relieves some of the pressure, but the farther I walk, the tighter my boot feels and the more my ankle aches. Freezing winds begin to blow hard against me.

I struggle around a curve and see crooked headstones sticking out of the snow. I step in a rut. My ankle turns and I drop right in my tracks. I lay still and wait for the throbbing pain in my ankle to stop. The wind whips around me sending a blast of snow up under my face shield. It feels like a slap in the face. Startled, I move too quickly and give my ankle another painful jolt. The pain is one too many.

"Okay God—I give up—I can't do this any more," I moan. "I am so tired of hurting. Why don't you just kill me, like you did my dad, and get it over with?"

I close my eyes and try to will the pain away. I wonder what it would be like to see my dad again. I am so exhausted—I have to rest—if only for a few minutes. I lay still and listen to the wind whipping around me.

After what seems only a moment, I open my eyes. I feel strangely refreshed and no longer cold. Gradually I set up and pull off my helmet. I must have slept a long time because it's dark and the night is clear and cool. The stars sparkle and the moon rays glimmer through the trees and glisten on the snow. The pine trees softly rustle in the breeze. I wish I could sit here forever surrounded by the beauty—it is so lovely and serene.

Then, I notice a path has been shoveled between the rows of headstones to the back of the cemetery where a faint light beckons to me. I stand up, cautiously take a step, and wonder why my ankle doesn't hurt. The thought quickly leaves as I realize the light is coming from a tiny glass window in a small cobblestone church I didn't even know existed.

Astonished, I walk quickly to the door. Without hesitation, I lift the wrought iron latch and step inside. I have never seen such a little church.

Directly in front of me three wooden pews stretch across the room, leaving a narrow aisle on each side. Facing the pews is a small pulpit, and behind that, a white wooden cross hangs on the stone wall. To the right of the pulpit, a fireplace burns. An aging, dark-skinned man dressed in old-fashioned clothes is putting wood on the fire. He turns and smiles at me.

"Good evening Chickadee," he says, "I've been waiting for you."

Chapter Four

I want to ask the man how he knows my name, but words fail me when a powerful warm circle of love floats around me. It seeps into my senses and deep into my pores. I close my eyes and stand motionless—welcoming it in. Love flows to the very core of my being, filling me like a sponge that has been dry too long. Love so strong that without a doubt—I know it is God. And I know for certain God loves me—has always loved me.

All the hateful things I thought and said these last months about God and His son Jesus flash through my mind. Tears spring forth as guilt and shame mingle with the flowing love. I say a silent prayer: Lord, please forgive me. I am so sorry.

As I stand there, a layer of heaviness gently lifts off my body and relief sweeps through me. In an instant I know I am forgiven. How incredible God is! How awesome His love!

I open my eyes and see the man is still smiling at me. I wonder if he knows what I am feeling.

"There's so much love in here," I barely whisper.

"It is the presence of God that you feel. Come, bask in His glory." The man motions to the pew closest to him.

I seem to float in slow motion as I cross the room and sit softly on the pew.

"Who are you?" I ask.

"Folks around here call me Preacher Joe."

He stretches to put another log on the fire. His shirt sleeve slides up his arm and I see deep scars circling his wrist. He turns and looks directly at me. I am amazed by the kindness I see in his eyes.

"Do you know Jesus, Chickadee?" he asks.

His directness surprises me.

"Yes...no...well, maybe." I stumble over the words. Then I look deep into his eyes and know I need to speak the truth.

"I mean—I thought I knew Jesus," I say. "I invited Him into my life. But, I don't know Him like my dad did. My dad would practically glow when he talked about Jesus. He would say, "God is love, love, love—nothing but love—and Jesus is the greatest love of all.""

"Your dad was right," Preacher Joe says. "Jesus walked this earth as a man so He knows exactly what it's like to live here, and in His death, He took our sins upon Himself, so that we who believe in Him shall have everlasting life. What greater love could there be?"

"But Jesus is supposed to be the healer and He let my dad die." Even with all the love flowing in and around me, saying the words causes a pain to shoot through my heart. "Jesus could have healed him right then and there if He had wanted to, but He didn't. He just left him to die all alone. I don't understand. My dad really loved Jesus, so why didn't He help him?"

Preacher Joe steps back and sits on the edge of the hearth. He folds his hands in his lap and I notice there are scars on his other wrist also.

"My dear child," he says, "Some questions have no answers. Knowing and loving Jesus, doesn't mean a long life, for we never know when death will come. Death comes to people of all ages. Your dad lived every day with joy in his heart because he knew and loved Jesus. Your dad was never alone. Jesus was with him when he lived and when he died."

"But what about me? Doesn't Jesus care about me? My heart aches every time I think about my dad. Doesn't that matter to Jesus?"

"Jesus knows the pain you feel, Chickadee. He understands your anger. The loss of your dad is hard to bear alone. Jesus loves you and wants to comfort you."

"Then, why doesn't He?" I can hear the anguish in my voice. "Is it because I blamed Him for letting my dad die?"

"Did you ask Jesus?"

"What do you mean?"

"Did you choose to ask Jesus to help you through your sorrow?"

"Well...no. I never thought about it. After He let my dad die, I didn't think He cared."

"Chickadee, we each choose what to think and what to do. God has given us choice in all matters. Jesus waits patiently at the door of our hearts, hoping we will choose Him to help us through our troubles. All we need to do is ask."

"But I didn't know His—His love before. I never felt anything like it."

I slump down in the pew. Tears stream down my face and I start to sob uncontrollably. It's true what Preacher Joe said: people do die at all ages. And I should have prayed to Jesus to help me, not blame Him. That is what my dad would have wanted me to do. I hope it's not too late. I start to pray:

Oh Jesus, I'm so sorry I turned away from You. I just didn't understand before. Please forgive me. Please help me. I want You in my life. I want to know You like my dad did.

Again, I feel overwhelming love surround me. This time invisible arms wrap around me and peacefulness and love—like I've never known before—fills my heart.

Deep inside, I know I am going to be okay. I close my eyes as the tears stream down my face. I silently thank Jesus over and over as wave after wave of His love washes through me.

"Rest now, child," I hear Preacher Joe say as he pats me gently on the head.

Chapter Five

Soft whispers float in the air around me. I crack open my eyes and find myself looking straight into the beautiful blue eyes of Harold Barnes. I'm dreaming—I must be dreaming. Standing next to him is Marcy and her mother Martha, then my mother and Stanley. They are all curved right around the bed I am laying on. Holy smokes! This is no dream. I sit straight up—wide awake—and we all start talking at once.

"What's going on in here?" Dr. Moore's gruff voice booms out over ours as he walks into the hospital room. "Sounds like some of my family gatherings. This young lady has had a rather rough night for so much chatter. Now if all of you will excuse us," he says glancing around the room, "I'd like to check on our patient here."

Harold smiles as he turns to leave and suddenly I realize my hair must be sticking out in all directions—as it is every morning. I try to smooth the tangled mess by combing my fingers through the long dark strands. What's he doing here anyway?

Marcy reaches over to give me a hug and whispers she will be right back.

Martha hugs me too, while Mother grabs Stanley by the arm and drags him around the end of the bed.

"We're going to breakfast," she informs me, "When I come back, I expect an apology." She turns and Stanley follows her out the door.

"Martha, wait a minute," I hear her call down the hall to Marcy's mom. "Would you like to join us for coffee?"

That's a surprise. Mother's never goes out of her way to be nice to Martha. I wonder what she's up to. I know one thing though, Mother can expect an apology all she wants, but she won't get it. I don' have anything to apologize for.

Dr. Moore walks over to the bed.

"How did I get here?" I ask, "The last thing I remember is sitting in the church in the woods."

"Church?" Dr. Moore says. "There is no church where you were. You must have been dreaming. That Barnes boy found you laying in the snow, disoriented and half frozen. You're lucky he came along, young lady—he probably saved your life. Now let me have a look at you."

Dr. Moore doesn't have to ask me to open my mouth to look down my throat, it just falls open at the thought of Harold Barnes saving my life. I can't remember a thing beyond sitting in the church. I search my mind for memories as Dr. Moore examines me from head to toe.

"Well, young lady," Dr. Moore says, "I'm amazed at how well you're doing this morning. There doesn't seem to be a thing wrong."

"Then can I go home?" I ask, wondering if I really want to.

"I can't see any reason to keep you here. I'll send the nurse in to see to you. Now you take care of yourself and don't do anything so foolish again. You might not be so lucky next time, young lady." Dr. Moore makes a note on his chart and shuffles out of the room.

Marcy peeks around the corner of the door. She grins and tilts her head causing the sun shining through the window from across the hall to dance like fire through her curly red hair.

"Well, young lady," she says, doing a poor imitation of Dr. Moore, "Would you like some company?"

"Sure would, young lady." I chuckle and pat the side of the bed. "Now get in here."

"Chickadee, look at you—you're almost laughing!" Marcy exclaims with a big smile.

"I guess I am. But I'm confused. Dr. Moore said Harold found me in the snow and saved my life. I can't remember anything beyond sitting in the church."

"Church? What Church?" Marcy has the same look of surprise as Dr. Moore.

"I found a church in the woods behind the cemetery."

"Chickadee, you know there's no church out there. You must have been dreaming."

"That's what Dr. Moore thinks," I say. Maybe they are right. I know there isn't a church in the woods, but—there must be—I was in it, so it couldn't have been a dream. It was all too real not to have been real.

"So tell me about it," Marcy drags the chair to the side of the bed and flops down.

"What?" I say, struggling with my thoughts.

"The dream, silly."

"First, tell me how I got here."

"Well, Harold was snowmobiling with his friend John—who is really cute by the way—when he saw a strange object in the snow. He swung by to check it out and it was you. He tried to get you up, but you were too weak. So, he sat in the snow and wrapped his arms around you to keep you warm while John went for help. He said you kept mumbling something about being sorry and thanking him. That's all I know, Chickadee."

"Harold Barnes held me in his arms?" My heart actually skips a beat. "It hardly seems fair that I can't remember it."

"Never mind that Chickadee, what were you doing way out there by yourself?"

"I had an argument with Mother—I actually yelled at her. I was so upset, I couldn't stand to be around her so I took off on the

23

snowmobile. I didn't think about checking the gas or anything. I just had to get away from her."

"So what did you fight about?" Marcy asks.

"Stanley Hood, of course. Mother says she's going to marry that jerk. And worse, she plans on selling our house and we have to live with him."

"Oh no," Marcy says, her face filling with sadness. "That is awful."

It always amazes me how Marcy's face can change from happy to sad in two seconds. "She's like an open book," my dad would say. But I know it's because she cares so much.

"They haven't known each other very long," Marcy adds. "Maybe they will stay engaged for a long time—and then maybe she will change her mind."

"I don't think so. She's talking about having a big yard sale this Spring. She's getting rid of everything that is connected to my dad! How could she? I hate her! And I know one thing else for sure—she hates me!"

"Oh no, Chickadee, don't say that. It's a terrible thing to hate. And she couldn't possibly hate you—you're her daughter." Marcy looks like she is ready to cry.

"Marcy, it's all right—really. It's a relief not to have to pretend any more that Mother likes me. Listen, I want to apologize for hanging up on you. You're my best friend and I wouldn't have been able to get through all these months without you. I am really sorry. I haven't been very nice."

"Oh Chickadee, I'm sorry too. I shouldn't have pushed you so hard."

Marcy reaches over and we hug and her smile comes back just as the nurse walks in with a tray of food. She sets it on the sliding table and pushes it in front of me.

"Here you go," she says. "It's not too bad for hospital food." She winks at me and smiles.

"Good because I'm hungry—but hey—I'm used to eating at school, and nothing can be as bad as school food."

"How well I remember," The nurse says. "Speaking of school—shouldn't you be there right now?" she says to Marcy.

"I had to take the day off," Marcy says with a grin. "My friend needs me."

"Well, good news then—you'll be able to make it tomorrow because the doctor is letting your friend go home. Now, let me get this IV out of your arm, Chickadee."

She walks around the bed to the machine where the plastic bag of liquid hangs from a pole and slowly drips down the tube into my arm. She fiddles with the machine, removes the tape from my arm and effortlessly slides the needle out.

"That was easy," I say, as she tapes a cotton ball on my arm over the spot where the needle was. "I thought it was going to hurt."

"Not a chance." The nurse flashes another smile. "We know what we're doing around here. Now, enjoy your breakfast and when your mom gets here send her to the nurses station. We have paperwork for her to sign before you're released."

"I've already signed it." Mother bristles into the room and drops a bag, her coat, and purse at the foot of the bed.

"Then my work's done here," the nurse says and pats my hand.

"That was a quick breakfast," I say to Mother as the nurse leaves.

Mother grabs up her purse and digs out a comb.

"We only went downstairs to the cafeteria. Now hurry up and finish your breakfast—we have a lot to do today," she says stepping into the bathroom.

She doesn't even bother to ask me how I feel so I make a face behind her back. Then, in deliberate slow motion pile scrambled eggs on a piece of toast and take a tiny, tiny bite. Marcy giggles then quickly covers her mouth, and glances towards the bathroom.

I start to take another tiny bite to see if I can get Marcy to giggle again, but I'm too hungry and bite off a big chunk instead.

"This is pretty tasty." I say opening up the small carton of milk. "Marcy do you want some? There's plenty. How about a dish of fruit or piece of bacon?"

"Sounds good, but I probably should get going, Chickadee," Marcy pushes herself up out of the chair.

Marcy's not comfortable around Mother, so I can't blame her for leaving. If only Mother could be more like Marcy's mom. When Marcy and I became best friends in the second grade she invited me to spend the night. It was the first time I met her mom and I called her Mrs. Meadows. She squatted down in front of me and smiled and said to call her Martha—then gave me a big hug. It made me feel so special and welcome. I'll never forget it.

"You're staying right here Marcy," Mother says, sticking her head out of the bathroom and waving a tube of lipstick in the air. "I told Martha, I'd bring you home."

Marcy sighs and sits back down.

"Well, in that case I'll have the fruit," she says, "I haven't eaten today either."

"Dig in." I say and slide the dish over and hand her the spoon.

"Your clothes are in the bag," Mother says, "When you get dressed, we're going back to the house and Marcy can help you pack up some things. You won't be living at home for a while."

Marcy and I stop eating and look at each other. She flips her hair back over her shoulder and sends me her it-will-be-okay-don't-worry-look, but it doesn't help. My stomach lurches and rolls into a knot—so much for breakfast.

"Well where am I going to live?" I snap and throw the toast back on the tray.

"Stanley has this great opportunity at work." Mother steps out of the bathroom while smoothing down her blouse to erase the imaginary wrinkles. "And he—"

"Why does everything have to be about Stanley." I practically shout. "I don't care about Stanley!"

"You know what Chickadee, I have had enough of your rotten attitude. I'm getting the car. Get your stuff together and meet me out front." Mother swings around and grabs her coat. "We'll discuss this at the house." She snatches her purse from the bathroom and stomps out of the room.

Chapter Six

The inside of the car is like a tomb. Mother—hunching forward with her hands clamped to the steering wheel—stares straight ahead. Marcy sits in the back seat quiet as a church mouse. If I hadn't seen her get in the car, I wouldn't know she was here. I'm like a statute, but my mind is anything but still.

The words,"You won't be living at home," repeat and race around in my head, dredging up all kinds of ugly scenarios. I see Mother locking me away in a reform school or some other place they stick troubled teens. She and Stanley will be off some where living happily together—I'll be tucked away in some horrible fenced-in building with a bunch of drugheads and violent gang members.

Preacher Joe said, "God gives us choice in all matters." I want to believe it, but I don't see as I have much choice in anything that matters. Mother is the one who gets to make all the choices and I have to go along with whatever she chooses. It's way too confusing to think about right now.

I reach over and turn the radio on. Mother pushes my hand away and immediately snaps it off.

"Leave it alone," she growls.

My stomach twists tighter in a knot. I wonder how it can be hungry and hurt at the same time. I hope I am too young to get an ulcer. I quietly slip my hand under my coat and rub my stomach.

Finally our house comes into view. Mother pulls in the driveway and stops.

She jumps out of the car and slams the door behind her.

"Wow," Marcy whispers. "I've never seen her so angry. Where do you think she plans to send you?"

"Who knows—I never can guess what she's thinking."

"She sure can be unpredictable," Marcy says, getting out of the car. "Maybe she's just trying to scare you. Maybe if you apologize she will say she didn't mean it."

"Maybe, but I think she would have dropped you off at your house before bringing me home if she didn't mean it. She said she wants you to help pack—remember? Let's just go in and get it over with."

Marcy takes a hold of my arm and gives it a squeeze.

"Whatever happens, God will make it okay, Chickadee."

We walk in the house with Marcy still holding onto my arm. Without a word, we shed out coats and boots. We find Mother pacing the livingroom.

"Sit down," she says.

Marcy quietly sits on the end of the couch while I flop down on the other end and brace my feet on the edge of the coffee table.

"Now," Mother instructs, "I don't want you to say one word until I am done speaking. Is that clear?"

I fold my arms over my hurting stomach and half nod my head. From the corner of my eye, I see Marcy chewing on her fingernail. She half nods too.

"As I started to say before," Mother says, perching on the edge of the chair, "Stanley's insurance company is opening a new office in Hawaii. He is flying down there for four weeks and has asked me to join him." She shoots me an icy stare. "If you hadn't acted so childish I would have been able to explain this before. Whether you like it or not, Chickadee, Stanley is an important part of my life."

"Now," she says, pausing long enough for my stomach to tighten another notch, "I am going with him. I spoke with Martha and have made arrangements for you to stay with her and Marcy while I am gone."

I look at Marcy to see if she heard what I heard. The look on her face tells me she did. I can't conceal the huge sigh of relief coming out of me. Thank you, God! Not in a million years would I have guessed this could happen. Maybe Mother doesn't hate me. Maybe I should apologize to her. I search my mind for the right words, but I can't remember what I am suppose to apologize for so I don't say anything.

"That's great Mrs. Bird." Marcy says, coming to the rescue. "We'll have so much fun. I hope you have fun in Hawaii, too."

"That's very nice of you to say, Marcy," Mother's voice softens a bit, "But, I'm not finished. Stanley and I leave for the airport early in the morning—so Chickadee—you need to pack some clothes and make sure you get all of your school books together. I told Martha I would drop you two off early so get a move on."

Marcy and I jump up and thunder up the stairs to my room. Marcy shuts the door behind us.

"I am so relieved," she squeals, "I have to admit, I was afraid you were going to be sent off some where to live with distant relatives."

"I was thinking all kinds of terrible things—but I don't know any distant relatives. My mother said she left her family in New Mexico and that is where they can stay. My dad had a sister, but she died when she was young and he wouldn't ever talk about her. Thank God I've got you, Marcy—you're like a sister."

"Yeah, and now we can live like sisters for four whole weeks. I'm so excited."

"I love staying with you and Martha. We always have so much fun together. I have missed coming over so much." I jump up on the bed and bounce up and down.

"Thank you God," Marcy says, smiling her biggest smile.

"Yes, Thank you God," I jump back down.

31

"Does this mean you aren't angry at God any more, Chickadee."

"It sure does! I learned that God loves me, Marcy. I mean, really loves me."

We laugh and hug and dance around the room. Marcy's face is beaming.

"So, tell me what happened," she says.

"I'm dying to tell you everything—all about the church in the woods—but we better wait until later. Let's get this stuff packed up so we can get out of here before Mother changes her mind."

"I agree," she says.

We scurry around and throw everything we think I can use into two bulging suitcases, one overnight bag and my school backpack. We drag them all downstairs.

"Is that everything?" Mother asks. She winds the cord around the vacuum cleaner and shoves it back in the closet.

"Just about." I run up the stairs, grab my dad's old flannel shirt from under my pillow, race back down and stuff it in my overnight bag.

"Can I help you do anything, Mrs. Bird?" I hear Marcy ask.

"No," Mother says, "I think I'm about done."

"Do you need me to do anything while you are gone?" I say, wanting to sound helpful, too.

"Yes I do," Mother says. "I'd like you to stop by a couple times a week to make sure the furnace is still running and everything is okay. If anything should go wrong, have Martha call me and I'll figure out what to do. But, I don't think there will be any problems."

"I can do that," I say. "I'll ride the bus home after school, check on everything, and walk over to Marcy's."

"I'll come with you," Marcy says, "It will be good exercise for us—if it's not too cold. You're the one who loves winter. I like the warmer weather, myself."

"I'm with you Marcy," Mother says, giving us a rare smile. "I am ready to be on the warm sunny beaches of Hawaii with Stanley."

With Mother smiling, I figure it is as good a time as any to work in the apology she wants. After all, she's letting me stay with Marcy for a whole month, plus I won't have to worry about doing it when she gets back.

"Mother," I say, "Thanks for letting me stay with Marcy." I know I should look at her, but I find myself staring at the suitcases on the floor. My heart picks up a beat. I wish I could know what she expects me to say. I bend down and give the suitcases a shove closer to the door.

"I'm sorry if I was disrespectful," I finally manage as my heart jumps full steam ahead. I take a deep breath and brace myself for a lecture about being nicer to Stanley. I hope I'm too young for a heart attack. An ulcer and a heart attack in the same day—how bad would that be.

"Apology accepted," Mother says simply. "Now you two get this stuff loaded in the car. I'll get my keys and meet you there."

"Whew," I whisper to Marcy as Mother walks away. "That was easy. "

"You did good," she whispers back.

Chapter Seven

"Come in—come in," Martha lunges forward and grabs a hold of me before I can step through the doorway. The familiar warmth of the house and the inviting smells of home cooking flowing from behind her suddenly make me realize how much I have missed Martha. I drop the suitcases and fling my arms around her. After my dad died, Marcy invited me over several times and every time I would say "no," and had to see the hurt look on her face until one day I couldn't stand to see it any longer and told her the truth: I was afraid to leave the house. It was embarrassing to admit—even to Marcy—how Mother seemed to enjoy clearing out Dad's belongings while I was gone. So many things began to disappear that I started squirrelling some of his stuff away in my room. Only since Stanley came along has Mother lost interest in what was left.

Other than going to school—because I had no choice—I was only able to leave the house a couple of times to snowmobile with Marcy while Mother was out with Stanley. I made sure I was back in the house before she got there. Oh how different my life would be if Martha was my mother. I squeeze her harder.

"I am so glad you are all right," Martha says, giving me a kiss on the cheek. "You gave us a scare last night."

"I know—what I did was stupid," I say not letting go of her. "I'm sorry I couldn't come over before."

"Marcy explained and I understand. I want you to know, Chickadee, this will always be your home away from home. Don't you forget it."

"Hey, it's cold out here." Marcy gives me a nudge in the back. "Can we continue this love-fest inside where it's warm?"

"Good idea," Martha says. She lets go of me and picks up one of the suitcases. I pick up the other and we all shuffle inside. Martha sets the suitcase by the stairs and moves over to the stove. She stirs a pot that smells so good, my stomach growls.

"Are you girls hungry?" she asks.

"Starving," we both say at once and high-five each other. We always do that when we say the same thing at the same time.

I hang up my coat and reach in the pocket and pull out an envelope.

"Before I forget—this is for you Martha," I lay the envelope on the counter next to a yummy looking cake. "Mother says it has a list of phone numbers and other information you might need."

"Okay," she says, "I'll look at it later. Why don't you sit down while I dish us up some good old homemade chicken soup. We'll worry about getting you unpacked later. It's been a long time since the three of us have had a chance to sit, relax, eat and chat. I've been looking forward to it all day."

How much I have missed hearing that!—"Sit, relax, eat and chat!" It kind of describes Martha's whole personality. I don't think anything makes her happier than having people around—except feeding them.

"Hey, I see you made my favorite cake with peanutbutter frosting." Marcy says, pulling a bag of oyster crackers out of the cupboard. "It is chocolate, isn't it?"

"Yes my darling daughter, now sit down so we can eat." Martha set three big steaming bowls of soup on the table. She reaches in the refrigerator and pulls out a container of milk and fills our glasses.

Marcy slides in the chair across from me, while Martha squeezes in between us and reaches for our hands.

"Thank you Lord for giving us this day our daily bread—as You do every day," Martha prays. "And thank You especially for watching over Chickadee and keeping her safe through the night. We are grateful to have her here with us. In Jesus's name, we pray. Amen."

Suddenly, I feel overwhelmed by how much they care for me and a tear trickles down my cheek.

Martha and Marcy both jump up from the table and circle around me. Martha pulls a tissue from the box on the counter and hands it to me.

"It will be all right, Chickadee," Marcy says with tears in her eyes. "We love you."

"I know you do and I love you guys." I wipe my eyes. "I don't know why I'm crying. I'm really happy to be here."

"Well, let's think about this for a moment," says Martha, "First you find out your mother's getting married and you argue with her, then you're stuck in the woods and nearly freeze to death, then you're rescued and spend the night in the hospital for observation, and now you've moved in with us. And all this in two days. Honey, I think that is enough stress to make any one weepy."

"I guess so—and it has tired me out." I manage a weak smile. "But, I think I have enough energy left to eat some of your great soup."

"Well, okay then—" Martha pats me on the shoulder. "God has a way of working things out, Chickadee, don't you worry." She squeezes back in her seat.

"That's right," Marcy adds. "He does. Now, pass me the crackers."

I eat two big bowls of soup while Marcy and her mom do most of the chatting. By the time the chocolate cake is cut, my stomach is feeling a whole lot better and the rest of me with it.

"I think it's getting cooler in her," Martha says, rubbing her arms. She walks over to the thermostat on the wall and pushes it up a notch.

"I hear we could have some freezing rain tonight and maybe tomorrow, too."

"I hope not," I say, "I don't want Mother to miss her plane."

"Yeah, but if we do get it," Marcy says, "We won't have to go to school."

"Either way, we have no control over the weather." Martha says, "So let's curl up in the livingroom and relax next to the fireplace with a cup of hot chocolate and not worry about it."

"Sounds good to me," I say, suppressing a yawn, "I want to tell you what amazing thing happened to me in the woods."

"First, I say we get our pajamas on and really get comfortable," Marcy says.

"You two do that and I'll make the hot chocolate," Martha says, slipping on a sweater.

I pick up my overnight bag and follow Marcy up the stairs. Five minutes later, we're sinking back into the soft cushions of the couch. Marcy reaches over to the rocking chair and pulls the folded afghan off the back of it. She tosses one end over me and curls up under the other.

"This is so pretty and soft," I say, running my hands over the colorful squares, "—and cozy."

"Here you go." Martha hands me and Marcy an oversized mug of hot chocolate and goes back to the kitchen and brings one out for herself. She sets it next to her recliner and adds another log to the fire.

"There, that's better," she says, as the flames flicker. She walks to the hall closet and pulls out an afghan with a beautiful intricate zig-zag design in shades of blues, greens, and yellows. She tucks it around her as she settles in the recliner.

"Martha, will you teach me to crochet sometime?" I ask, "These afghans are so beautiful. I would love to learn how to make one."

"Why, I would like that very much, Chickadee—whenever you are ready." She takes a sip of hot chocolate. "Now, tell us what happened to you in the woods."

Chapter Eight

"I guess you know the part where Harold found me laying in the snow in front of the old cemetery." I reach over to the end table and set the mug of hot chocolate on the crocheted coaster.

"Well, when the snowmobile quit, I kicked it and hurt my ankle— I know it was a stupid thing to do—but I was angry. Then I started walking and putting pressure on my ankle and it started to swell. By the time I made it back to the old cemetery, it was hurting pretty bad. Then, I stepped into a rut and fell and twisted it. Boy…did that ever hurt. I was so tired and in so much pain. I only meant to lay still until my ankle quit throbbing, but when I opened my eyes it was dark."

"Anyway, I saw a path between the headstones and a light at the back of the cemetery. God must have healed my ankle because— when I stood up—it didn't hurt. Isn't that amazing?"

Marcy and Martha shake their heads in agreement.

"It truly is—," Martha says. "Then what happened?"

"I followed the path to the small cobblestone church. It had a heavy wooden door with a little square window and a big black wrought iron door latch. I went inside and a man was standing by the fireplace. He wore old-fashioned clothes and said his name was Preacher Joe. We talked and the last thing I remember was sitting in one of the pews. I haven't a clue as to how I got back out in the snow where Harold found me."

"That's why it sounds like a dream," Marcy says.

"If it was a dream, wouldn't my ankle still hurt?"

"I don't know," Marcy says, "but you know there really isn't a church in the woods."

"I know that up here," I say pointing to my head, "But, down here"—I point to my heart—"I know there was. And that's what so puzzling. I keep thinking about it and it sounds crazy to say the church was there—but it must have been—because it was so real."

"What made it so real?" Martha asks.

"God did," I say without hesitation. "The most amazing thing happened when I walked through the door. I felt God's love fill me. It flowed all over me, around me, and through me. It was incredible. I knew then that He loves me. I mean He really loves me. And, I learned there's a difference between thinking He does and knowing it. And then, Preacher Joe started talking to me and I started praying and crying and asking God and Jesus to forgive me and to help me. And—oh—I actually felt Jesus wrap His arms around me and fill me with His peace and love. I never felt anything like it in my life. It's like I'm a new person."

I look from Marcy to Martha, and back again.

"Well, there is something different about you," Marcy says. "I noticed it in the hospital. You don't seem to be depressed any more. And right now when you were talking, your eyes were shining just like your dad's use to do when he talked about Jesus."

"They sure were," Martha says. "Tell us what you and Preacher Joe discussed."

"Well, the thing that sticks with me most is that he said: 'We each choose what to think and what to do and that God has given us choice in all matters.' And, he asked me if I chose to ask Jesus to help me through my sorrow. I hadn't—but it got me thinking. That is what my dad would have wanted me to do—instead of being angry. So, I prayed and told Jesus I was sorry I turned away from Him and I asked Him to help me and that's when I felt His arms wrap around me. I will never forget that feeling. What do you think, Martha? Do you think it could have been a dream?"

"Well, we know there isn't a church out there now," she says carefully. "But maybe there was at one time. Perhaps God made it appear real for you because you needed for it to be there. I think He has given you a vision or special healing of sorts—physical and spiritual."

"You mean like a miracle?" Marcy asks.

"Maybe…" Martha says looking at me, "If you felt the power of God's love so strong that it has healed you in any way—well, I guess it would be considered one."

"All I know is how real it was to me, and—church or dreamed-up church—God touched my heart and I am different."

"Mom," Marcy says. "When you go into the Library to work tomorrow, why don't you ask the research lady if she has any history about Cemetery Ridge. If there ever was a church there she would know."

"Good idea Marcy," I say. "And if there ever was—I know what it looked like.

"I have another good idea," Martha says. She gets up and disappears around the corner of the kitchen to the dining area she turned into her at-home office. She comes back with a notebook in her hand.

"Here," she says, handing it to me. "I think you should write down everything you can remember about last night. Journaling is a great way to sort out your thoughts and feelings. It's especially helpful when something so powerful happens in your life."

"Mom gave me a notebook to write in after your dad died. It does help. I miss him too, you know. " Marcy says. "But the hardest thing for me has been to see you so hurt and sad all this time. I've missed us not spending time together and mostly I just missed you being you."

"I've missed me being me too, Marcy." I slide over and put my arm through hers. "But, I am going to be okay now—I just know it."

Chapter Nine

The aroma of coffee drifts up the stairway, winds into Marcy's bedroom, and up my nose. How can anything smell so good and taste so bad? I stretch and yawn and look out the window. Marcy got her wish—ice is every where. Even the fence at the edge of the lawn has icicles hanging from it. Tree limbs are coated and bending down. The big spruce tree by the mailbox has branches sagging to the ground. The mail box itself, looks as if it will have to be chiseled open. It all makes me smile. If the sun decides to peek through the clouds it will be a sparkling paradise.

I glance at the clock. Wow! Almost nine o'clock. I jump up, pull some clean clothes out of my suitcase and step around the corner to the bathroom. I hear the phone ring over muffled voices downstairs as I turn on the shower. If Martha is home, the Library is closed—everything must be closed. I expect Mother is having a fit because she's not on the plane to Hawaii.

It's not long before I'm drying off. I throw on a sweatshirt, a pair of jeans, and pull my hair back into a pony tail. I find my socks and follow the smell of bacon.

"Good morning," I say, popping around the corner of the stairs. "It's smelling good in here."

"Well, good morning to you." Martha says, "Did you have a good sleep?"

"She sure did," Marcy says. "She snored all night." She flips a pancake over in the pan and shoots me a grin.

"Well if I did it sure worked—I feel great today." I grin back at her and slide the chair out from the table. I reach down and pull on my socks. "Have you got my breakfast ready yet?"

"I did have, but you slept so late that it got cold and I had to throw it out to the birds. Sorry—these pancakes are for me."

"Yeah, well, I'm a Bird. I'll just go out there and join them."

"You girls and your banter!" Martha laughs, "How I have missed it."

"Me too," Marcy and I say at once and laugh. I jump up and we high-five each other.

"I'll set the table," I say, maneuvering around Martha to the dish cupboard.

"Guess who called?" Marcy says in a sing-songy voice.

"Mother."

"No…Harold," Martha says, and I almost trip over myself. "He wanted to tell you he brought your snowmobile back to your house and all it needed was some gas. Apparently your mother told him you were here. I think that boy likes you, Chickadee."

"He sure does," Marcy says. "He stayed all night at the hospital waiting for her to wake up."

"Yeah—and don't forget he saved my life." I set the plates on the table and add the napkins and silverware. I think about Harolds beautiful blue eyes. I haven't felt so happy in a long time.

"Martha, before I went to sleep last night, I wrote everything I can remember in the notebook you gave me. I decided to call it my *God Journal* because I am writing to God in it."

"That's great," Martha says, pouring coffee in her mug.

"Yeah—it will be like saying a prayer every time you write in it." Marcy adds. She slides the plate of bacon over and adds a heaping plate of little round pancakes to the table.

We sit down and Martha takes our hands.

"I want to say the prayer this time," I say.

"Thank you God for letting me be here with Marcy and Martha. Thank you for the food we have to eat and bless those that don't have any. Watch over us and keep us safe. Oh, and thank you for winter and the beautiful icy day. Amen."

"Very nice," Martha says and reaches for a pancake. "I have a project planned. I was going to bring it up this weekend, but seeing how we are housebound we can do it today."

"What?" Marcy and I say together and high-five each other across the table.

"Well, I was going to move things around in the sewing room so we could put the folding bed in there and Chickadee could have her own space while she's here."

"I don't mind sharing my room," Marcy says.

"I don't mind it either," I add.

"I know—but I know you girls too—and I can't have you talking and giggling all night every night. You need sleep for school and I need sleep for work. And as much as you enjoy being together, it's nice to be able to go to your own room."

"I guess you're right, Mom," Marcy teases. "Besides, you know how Chickadee snores." She laughs and takes a bite of bacon.

"Yeah…well…I agree too, Martha. After all, you know how Marcy talks in her sleep." I take a bite of bacon and laugh too.

"Oh my," Martha sighs, "It's going to be a long four weeks." She shakes her head and takes a bite of bacon. We all laugh.

We finish breakfast and Marcy and I clean up the kitchen while Martha putters in her sewing room. I glance out the window. No sunshine yet. Just dull grey overcast sky—but the ice is still there—waiting for the sun too.

I follow Marcy up the stairs. At the landing is a wide open hallway. Across the hall on the right is Marcy's bedroom, and across the hall on the left is Martha's sewing room. Straight ahead is the bathroom. Around the stairway, past Martha's sewing room, there is a door at the end of the hall that leads to the attic. The door is open and we hear Martha grunt as she shoves something across the floor.

"Wait a minute, Mom," Marcy calls out, "We'll help you."

We run up the stairs to where the attic opens up into a long narrow room the length of the house. There is a window at each end of the room. The view outside both windows is almost completely blocked by huge icicles hanging from the roof. A dusty bare light bulb hangs from the middle of the room where the ceiling peaks, making it hard to tell if the walls are painted grey or just dirty. There's a large water stain down one side of the fireplace chimney where there must have been a leak at one time. The whole room is dirty and dusty and smells.

We find Martha leaning on an old trunk. We can see a trail of dust on the floor where she pushed it up against the wall under the window.

"Whew," Martha says, "That's heavier than I remember and just look at how dusty it is. Some day I'll have to get up here and clean this attic out."

Stuff is piled everywhere. In the middle of the room is a baby crib with a couple of old dolls perched in it. Two old dressers with peeling paint are next to the stairway rail. One wall has shelves built on it the length of the room and is loaded with odds and ends. A couple of broken end tables, an old lamp and odd shaped boxes are scattered about—all covered in dust and cobwebs.

"I don't know why I bothered to move this old trunk. I don't want to store any of my good sewing stuff up here in this mess—not even in plastic boxes," Martha says.

"It's a great attic, though," I say, "It looks like somebody was going to make a bedroom up here at one time."

"The people I bought the house from used it as an attic, but they told me the people before them were in the process of making it into a playroom for their kids when the husband was transferred. I suppose with lots of work, it could be made into a fairly descent room, but it's just a smelly old attic to me—a good place for storage."

"And, you know what a packrat Mom is," Marcy says. "Every time she is going to get rid of something she changes her mind because she thinks she might need it later on. It all ends up here. When is the last time you actually came up here to get something you needed, Mom?"

"Good heavens—I don't know that I ever have," Martha says brushing off the front of her shirt. Let's get out of this dusty old attic and back to the sewing room. We need a different plan."

Marcy and I follow her down the stairs. We walk in the sewing room and it suddenly lights up as the sun streams through the window.

"Wow...look outside," I say. "It's beautiful—everything sparkles!"

"Oh, it does...well, it did," Marcy says as the sun instantly disappears behind a cloud and it's a dull, grey day again.

"At least we got to see it," I say with a shrug.

"Back to work..." Martha says. "I think if I fold down the cutting table and we take those boxes of fabric and slide them under Marcy's bed, there might be enough space to put the bed up by the window. It won't give you lots of room, but it will be your own space."

"Maybe we could stack some fabric in here," I open the closet door and immediately erupt into laughter. "Holy cow, Martha, you have enough fabric in here to open your own store!"

"I know...I know, but when I quilt it seems I never have the right color or pattern I need and so,—well, it just accumulates."

"You should see Mom in the fabric shop." Marcy teases. "She practically drools."

"Hey, you two—it could be worse, you know." Martha pretends

she's offended. "I could have a passion for collecting live lizards or something crazy like that. How would you like to live with a houseful of them?"

"Oh Mom, you know I love fabric." Marcy says dramatically. She puts her arm around Martha and lays her head on her shoulder and giggles.

"And I love quilts." I add, "But, a pet lizard or two would be okay."

Chapter Ten

Dear God, I have been living with Marcy and Martha for three days and I am so happy here. Thank you for the special time I had with you in the church in the woods. I am feeling better about my dad and don't cry every time I think about him.

I think about what Preacher Joe said and I am trying hard to understand how I can have choice in all matters. Preacher Joe said we choose what to think and what to feel, but I thought it automatically happened. Please help me understand.

"Chickadee, are you coming?" Marcy calls for the third time. "This is important."

"Yep, I'll be right there." I close my journal and slip it under my pillow.

Marcy's sitting on her bed—her legs folded Indian style—filing her nails. I sit down on the bed across from her.

"Okay," I say. "Now what's so important?"

"Mom's birthday is in a couple of weeks and I have an idea. Why don't we clean out the attic for her as a present? I think she would like it. It would take some work, but if we clean it she can store her fabric there. What do you think?"

"I think it's a great idea. We could even paint it and decorate it and turn it into a big sewing room for her."

"Oh, that's even better!...Let's do it!" Marcy's face beams with joy—briefly—and then her worry look takes over. "Only one problem: how do we do it without her knowing what we're doing?

Plus, I wouldn't want to throw away anything she really wants to keep."

"Well, when she gets home from work, why don't we sit her down and tell her we want to clean the attic for her birthday—make her promise not to peek—and then on her birthday, the sewing room will be a surprise."

"Yeah, that would work. We could drag stuff down and she could look over the things before we throw them out. And, there is probably some things that could be stored in the garage."

Let's go check it out and see what ideas we can come up with," I say.

We jump up and hustle up the stairs. By the time we come back down our heads are swimming with ideas and we can't wait to get started.

"Martha is going to love it," I say.

"She sure will." Marcy says. "But right now we better get at our homework—you know Mom's going to ask when she gets home."

"Yeah, I have some crappy math to catch up on." I say making a face.

We grab our backpacks and head to the kitchen table. Marcy finishes her homework before me and decides to fix dinner.

"How about I make a big tossed salad?' she says, poking around in the refrigerator. "Hey, we've got some hot dogs. We can cook them in the fireplace. We haven't done that in ages. We'll have a winter picnic and then after we eat, we'll tell Mom about her birthday present."

"Too bad we don't have a piece of cake left to put a candle in."

"We could make some brownies," Marcy says. "I'm sure there is a mix in the cupboard. They don't take long to make."

"Okay, I'm done with my math." I slam the book shut. "I'll stir up the brownies while you make the salad." I reach for my backpack and cram my homework in it.

When Martha comes home, she walks in the door with a smile. "Yum...it smells mighty good in here," she says, giving us each a hug.

"We're planning a picnic in the livingroom, Mom. Will you start the fireplace so we can cook hot dogs?" Marcy asks.

"Sure will," Martha says, "I love hot dogs cooked over a real fire. And, I'm ready to sit, relax, eat and chat. It's been a long day. Did you girls get your homework done?"

"Yes," we both answer and high-five each other.

"Mom, you go start the fire and get comfortable and we'll bring dinner in. We're going to wait on you tonight," Marcy says.

"You won't get an argument from me." Martha picks up the envelope I had left on the counter. "I probably ought to open this," she says and takes it with her.

Marcy hands me a tray from the cupboard. I dig out the silveware, napkins and plates. I stack them on the tray along with three bottles of soda and a dish of potato chips. Marcy stacks another tray with the salad, hot dogs, mustard and a jar of pickles.

"We don't have any hot dog rolls, but we've got bread," she says adding a partial loaf to the tray.

"That will work," I say. "Don't forget the long skewers to cook the hot dogs."

"Got 'em right here. We'll come back later for the brownies. I'll fix a special one for Mom," she whispers.

Martha's sitting back in her recliner with her feet up and her eyes closed. The envelope lays on the end table next to her. We set our trays on the coffee table and sit on the floor in front of the fire.

"I'm not sleeping," she says, "...just resting. Cook my hot dog nice and dark, please."

Marcy puts two hot dogs on her skewer and I put one on mine. They sizzle and spit in the fire. My stomach growls.

"We've got salad and potato chips, Mom, "Marcy says.

"I see…it looks delicious and I'm hungry," Martha says. "By the way I talked to the historian at the Library and she never heard of a church up on Cemetery Ridge, but she is going to research it."

"I can't wait to hear what she finds," I say.

"Me either," says Marcy.

We finish cooking the hot dogs and settle around the coffee table. Martha says a prayer and we fix our plates. Everything tastes so good.

"Should we tell her now? Marcy asks, smiling ear to ear.

"What?" Martha asks, raising her eyebrows.

"Well, Chickadee and I have been talking and we thought that for your birthday we would clean out the attic."

"Oh my goodness," Martha says. "That would be wonderful, but are you sure? That is quite an undertaking."

"We have it all figured out," I say. "We'll clean and dust everything off and bring it down in boxes and you can decide what you want to keep."

"We can store some stuff, Mom, but I think we should throw a lot of things in the garbage. Or, maybe we should do what Chickadees mom is planning and have a yard sale."

"Maybe we should have a sale. I know there is a lot of stuff in the attic that I don't need, but it's hard for me to throw things away. I would be easier to sell it—if anyone would want it, that is."

"We can store boxes in the back of the garage until it's nice weather," Marcy says.

"Oh you girls are so thoughtful. What a nice birthday present this will be. But there is one thing I don't want you to disturb and that's the big trunk I moved under the window. It's full of keepsakes from my mother and grandmother. We'll go through it together some day."

"No problem," Marcy says. "We can work around it."

"And I have been wondering what I was going to do with you two

52

during winter break," Martha says, smiling. "Don't forget that starts Monday—cleaning the attic will probably take you all of the two weeks."

"Yeah, we were thinking that too, but it gives us something to do and it will be fun. Who knows what we will find hidden away up there." I laugh.

"Well, if you find gold up there, we'll split it three ways." Martha says.

"I'm going to get us some brownies," Marcy says. "I'll be right back."

Martha yawns and pushes back in her recliner.

I stack the trays together and load them up while Martha reaches for the envelope—tears it open and starts to read.

"I'll take this back to the kitchen and help Marcy," I say.

I stick the pickles and mustard back in the refrigerator and put the dishes in the sink.

"I'm ready," Marcy says, pushing a candle through whip cream piled high on top of a brownie. "Let's go."

Singing "Happy Birthday" we walk into the livingroom. We take one look at Martha's face and come to a stop.

"What's wrong, Mom?" Marcy says. She puts the brownie on the coffee table and sits next to her mom.

"That woman!" Martha shakes the paper she was reading in the air and slams it on the end table, knocking the envelope to the floor. "I should have opened this sooner. I'm sorry Chickadee, but I will never understand your mother! If she were here I would give her a good piece of my mind."

"Why—what happened? What did she say?" My legs start shaking and I feel sick to my stomach. I sit down on the couch. I hate that my mother upset Martha.

"I don't know any way to tell you this, Chickadee, but to come right out and say it. Your mother—that irresponsible excuse for a mother—has eloped!"

Chapter Eleven

"Eloped?…You mean she's married already?" I might throw up. I slowly stand but Martha motions me to sit back down. She takes a deep breath and I can see she is trying to calm herself.

"That's not all," she says. "There's more."

"Isn't that enough?" Marcy asks. She reaches over and takes my hand.

"It's more than enough," Martha says quietly.

"Well, what more is there?" I ask, "You might as well tell me now and get it over with."

"Your right Chickadee—it is what it is—and it has to be dealt with," Martha says, "I'll just read the letter and then we can discuss it."

> *Martha,*
>
> *I appreciate you taking in Chickadee while I am away. I have to confess though, I told a little white lie. I am going to Hawaii with Stanley, but we are getting married by the justice of the peace before we leave. Stanley's insurance company is opening their new office in Honolulu and he is transferring there.*
>
> *We will honeymoon for two weeks before he starts work. We will also be looking for a new home and hope to find a nice condo near the*

beach. I will be back in four weeks to clear out my house and put it on the market before returning to Hawaii with Chickadee.

I'm sorry to burden you with explaining this to Chickadee, but she's been rather difficult lately. She can't accept change well and does not listen to me. Perhaps she will listen better to you. In any event by the time I get back, I hope she will be through throwing a fit and will realize how lovely living in Hawaii will be.

I am enclosing a list of phone numbers if you need to reach me and also a check to you from Stanley for added expenses. Once again, I appreciate your help.

Robin

"I'm so sorry, Chickadee," Martha says, laying the letter down. "I know this must come as a shock to you."

It must be shock. My mind is blank—I can't speak—I can't think—I can't even cry. Somehow I manage to stagger up the stairs. Marcy and Martha are right behind me, talking to me all the way, but I can't register what they are saying. I fall face first on the bed. They both sit down and rub on my back and tell me they love me, but it doesn't help. Oh God, how can this be happening? I can't imagine living in a city, much less in Hawaii. It doesn't even snow in Hawaii—ever! I throw my arms around my pillow and my hands bump against my God journal. I think about what I wrote just a few hours ago about being happy. Mother says I can't accept change, but it is her changes I can't accept. Where are my choices, God? I try to connect to the love I felt in the church in the woods but my heart feels empty. The tears finally come and I turn my head and sob into the pillow.

Martha sticks a tissue in my hand and tucks a blanket around me.

"It will be okay, Chickadee," she whispers in my ear, "God will help you through this. You go ahead and cry out your emotions and get some rest. We will talk when you're ready. Marcy and I will be close by saying prayers for you."

"Come Marcy, let's go downstairs and let Chickadee have her privacy. She needs to cry this out."

I hear Martha quietly shut the door as they leave.

Oh God, why can't my mother love me as much as Martha and Marcy do?

I cry until my eyes hurt. I feel devestated—just like I did when my dad died.

Wait a minute! I *did* feel just like this. I sit up and wipe my eyes. I did everything wrong then—I am not going to do everything wrong again. I gaze out the window. The moon is beautiful and full. Light reflects on the icy patches left over from the storm. I lift the window and smell the cool fresh air. The snow banks plowed back along the edge of the road glisten. The big pine tree by the mail box has come unhinged from the ice and the branches brush against each other in the breeze. I push the window open farther and stretch to see the stars sparkling in the night sky. I feel my spirit lift.

"I do have a choice," I say out loud. I lean on the windowsill and feel the cool air caress my skin. I fold my hands in prayer.

"Dear Lord, Dear Jesus, I need you. I am hurting inside and even though I can't feel your love right now, I know it's there and I know it's real. So, I am choosing to believe You will help me to do whatever I have to do until I am old enough to make the choices that will make me happy. I can't think of anything worse than what my mother has chosen for me. I don't want to go to Hawaii and I sure don't want to live with Stanley. I am going to need You more than ever to help me get through this. I am going to love You and trust You no matter what happens, because like Marcy and Martha, I know You really love me. Thank you, Amen."

I take another deep breath of fresh air and close the window. After washing my face and combing my hair, I go downstairs. Martha and Marcy are sitting in front of the fireplace and they both look up at me.

"Wow…" Marcy says, "What happened? You look…well, you look…okay."

"Thanks," I say. "I am okay. Remember how I told you about Preacher Joe saying God gives us choices. Well, I finally figured out what he meant. I don't have a choice in what Mother chooses for my life, but I can choose my reaction to her choice. So I prayed and asked God to help me deal with whatever I have to deal with until I'm old enough to make my own choices about how and where I want to live."

"Very, very good, Chickadee," Martha jumps up and hugs me. "I am so proud of you."

"I am really trusting God to help me do what I have to do, because I don't want to be any where, but right here where I am— with the people who really love me."

"We have been thinking about that too," Martha says. "Marcy and I have been praying and talking about your situation. I'm pretty sure when your mother gets back, I can convince her to let you live with us at least until school is out for the summer. I'm sure she'd like some time alone with Stanley."

"Oh Martha, do you really mean it?"

"Of course I do." she says. "Now, give me another hug."

"See, God is good," Marcy says, flashing me her biggest smile.

"I say we not worry any longer about tomorrow until it gets here. Right now I have a birthday brownie floating in melted whipped cream waiting for me to enjoy," Martha says, reaching for it on the coffee table. "Are you girls going to join me?"

Chapter Twelve

Dear God, It's Friday and school is out for winter break— two whole weeks. Marcy's babysitting tonight for the Johnson twins. They are six years old and Marcy babysits every other Friday so Mr. and Mrs. Johnson can have a date night. Marcy says they go to dinner and a movie. She starts babysitting at seven and Jerry and Josey are already in their pajamas, so all she has to do is read them a couple of stories and tuck them in bed. Marcy loves being with them. I guess You know how big her heart is.

Anyway, I thought it might be a good time to ask Martha to teach me to crochet. She said I should start with something smaller than an afghan—like a scarf. She has a whole draw full of different color yarn. I picked a bright red with yellow flecks in it. Martha called it bulky yarn. Anyway I tried to do what she said, but my crocheting sure doesn't look like Martha's. I'm not giving up though—no matter how many times I have to start over.

I think so much about the church in the woods. It is hard to believe it doesn't exist because it was so real to me. I am trying to be smart about every choice I make. I choose not to think about Mother and Hawaii, but it's still in the back of my mind and sometimes before I know it—I'm thinking about it anyway. I believe You will be with me and help me no matter what happens, but I am praying with all my heart that I won't have to go to Hawaii. Please God, let me stay here.

I want to thank You for the fun Marcy and I had when we got off the bus today at my house. Walking back to Marcy's it started snowing—the great big soft snowflakes—my favorite! I think snowflakes are the most beautiful things You ever created. Marcy and I were catching them on our tongues. We were looking up, not paying attention to where we were going, and Marcy stepped on the edge of the ditch and lost her balance and slid down in. I had to help her out. Her pants were all wet and we laughed and laughed. It looked like she had an accident in them and she had to walk the rest of the way back to her house that way. When a car came by we would stop walking and I'd stand real close to her. She would turn around and face the car so no one could see her backside—then we would laugh again.

And thank you for having Harold standing around the hall corner at school so when Marcy and I turned the corner I smacked right into him. I thanked him for saving my life and for bringing my snowmobile back. I think my face got a little red, but I don't care, I can't help it 'cause I like him. He said he was going south to visit his grandparents during winter break and won't be back until school starts. Then he asked Marcy and me if we would like to go snowmobiling with him and John some time after that. Marcy and I said "sure" at the same time and high-fived each other. He smiled at me and told us to have a good winter break. He is just so darn cute—it's hard for me not to stare at him.

Martha has to work tomorrow so Marcy and I are going to get up early and start the attic project. Martha promised not to go up to the attic until we are done. She is going to stop after work tomorrow and get some extra boxes and then pick up a pizza on the way home.

It has been a busy day and night. I think I hear Marcy coming home, so I will say goodnight, God, and thank you for choosing to love me.

Chapter Thirteen

The second Martha shuts the door to leave for work, Marcy and I drag the vacuum cleaner, broom, handfull of rags, garbage bags, empty boxes, and a large wicker basket to the attic.

"Where shall we start?" I ask, looking over one pile to another.

"How about if you knock down the cobwebs with the broom and I run the vacuum cleaner behind you?" Marcy answers. "That way, we can clean without getting too dirty—or cobwebs in our hair."

"I definitely don't want cobwebs in my hair." I pick up the broom. Marcy plugs in the vacuum cleaner and follows me along as I sweep down the ceiling and walls. We get all the way around the outside and Marcy starts vacuuming the middle of the floor. I shove stuff this way and that so she can gather up as much dirt and dust as she can.

"Wow," she says, turning the vacuum cleaner off. "It looks better all ready. I didn't think the floor was this nice. If we scrub it—it might even be pretty."

"I think so too," I say, "At first I thought it was real hardwood flooring, but it's just made to look that way. Why don't we scrub it last and start cleaning the walls by the stairs and work our way along the shelves?"

"I like that idea," Marcy says, "Then we can use the shelves to set stuff on as we need to. Let's go get a couple buckets of soap and water." She shoves the vacuum cleaner out of the way."

By noon, we have the top shelf clear and clean. We stack the items we think Martha might want to keep in the wicker basket. Then we fill empty boxes with old canning jars, a few stray nails, a wall lamp, a small kitchen scale and other small odds and ends we were sure could go in the sale pile.

We carry the containers down the two flights of stairs and set them on the floor next to Martha's recliner and head to the kitchen for lunch.

Marcy gives her mom a call while I wash up. Martha insists we call her every day around noon when she's working and check in with her.

"I don't worry about you girls getting into trouble, I just like to know you're okay," she says.

"Yeah...we're doing fine, but we are going to need lots of boxes," I hear Marcy say. "Okay...we'll see you later...I love you too, bye."

"I'll make lunch while you wash your hands," I say. "How about a bologna and cheese sandwich?"

"Sounds good," Marcy says.

I put a couple of paper towels on the counter and make our sandwiches on them. The less dishes we dirty—the less we have to wash. I grab the partial bag of potato chips and two apples and set them on the table next to the sandwiches. I pour us each a glass of milk.

"We should be able to have all the shelves cleaned by the time Mom gets home," Marcy says sitting down at the table. "It's not going to take as long as we thought to clean—it's mostly dust. The only thing we are really going to have to scrub is the floor."

"I agree," I say. "I was thinking that when we get the baby crib washed down, we can put Martha's yarn in it—she'd have a big yarn bin."

"Oh...I like that thought. Mom wouldn't get rid of of the crib anyway—it was mine. She said she's keeping it for my babies some day."

"Oh yeah? Are you planning to have lots of babies?"

"Might—you just never know—but, not right away." Marcy chuckles. "Listen—we should be ready to paint by the middle of the week. I was wondering how much paint will cost. We can use the babysitting money I saved—but we have to buy the paint and get it here without Mom knowing."

"We might not need money. My dad has paint cans stacked up in one of the closets in our backroom. I bet we can find something there we can use. We could have your Mom drop us off after church tomorrow and check it out. Besides, I want to pick up my dad's Bible."

"Oh...I hope he has some nice colored paint stashed away," Marcy says, chomping on an apple.

"Me too," I say. "Mother never got as far as the backroom when she was throwing out Dad's stuff. He had paint brushes and rollers and everything we'll need. I think he would like us to use it."

"I think he would too," Marcy says, pushing her chair back from the table. She sets her glass in the sink. "So, are you ready to get back at it?"

"Yep," I say, wading up the paper towel. I finish my milk, rinse the glass and set it in the sink next to Marcy's. "Let's go."

"These stairs are good exercise," Marcy says, catching her breath at the top step. "Yuck," she adds, glancing at the buckets on the floor, "We should have taken those down with us and changed the water."

I look at the muddy mess.

"I guess we better do it now," I say and pick up a bucket. Marcy picks up the other and we go back down the stairs and haul up the clean soap and water.

Before long we run out of boxes to fill, so we clean off some of the bigger items and wrestle them down the two flights of stairs. We make several trips and make a pile at the back door and then put on our coats and truck it to the garage.

"I don't think Mom will want to keep any of this," Marcy says, looking over the broken end tables, broken wall mirror, and chair with only three legs. "I don't even know what those are for." She points at some long metal rods sticking out behind three rusty milk pails."

"I don't either. If Martha doesn't want to keep any of this we can put it out for the garbage man and get it out of here for good."

We make another trip to the attic to dust off and gather up an armload of boxed puzzles and board games and bring them down to the coffee table.

"Hello," we hear Martha say, "I'm home—anyone for pizza?"

"Yes!" Marcy and I say. We high-five each other and rush out to the kitchen.

"By the looks of the garage—you two have been busy." Martha puts the pizza on the counter and gives us each a hug.

"Wait until you see the livingroom," Marcy says with a grin.

"Yeah," I say, "You've got a lot of choices to make tonight."

Chapter Fourteen

Dear God, Marcy and I got a great start at cleaning out the attic yesterday. Martha brought home pizza—it was my favorite with lots of mushrooms and cheese.

After we ate, Martha looked over all that we brought down from the attic. She wanted to keep the puzzles and board games, but Marcy talked her into putting most of them in the sale pile. By the time Martha was through looking, Marcy had her talked into getting rid of almost everything. Martha wouldn't part with the canning jars, though. She said she just might want to can something some day, so Marcy gave in. Martha did agree the junk in the garage could go out for the garbage man. She said she had no idea why she kept such broken down things anyway.

I think Martha did really good because she is a packrat and it is hard for her to let things go.

I keep wondering what it will feel like to clean out the house with Mother. I'm like Martha and want to hang on to things that it probably doesn't make sense to. But if she can let things go— well, then, so can I. That is if you help me Lord. And, I know you will.

I want to keep a few things my dad had and I want to keep my chickadee ornaments and some other stuff in my room. I wish I could keep everything, but that would be crazy. I would end up with an attic someday like Marthas. And—like Martha

said last night, "It's just stuff—and material stuff isn't all that important." I'm glad Mother can't throw out my memories."
I better stop writing or I will be late getting dressed for church. I'll meet you there, God.

"So…how did it feel being back in church, Chickadee?" Marcy asks, as Martha backs the car out of the parking space.

"It felt good. I didn't realize how much I've missed going until I heard the choir sing. I love the hymns."

"I like the music too—it always lifts my spirit," Martha says. "Now, you two said you want me to stop at Chickadee's—do you want me to wait while you check on things?"

"Naw," I say, "We'll walk back—it's not too cold today." I glance at Marcy and she gives me her we-know-something-she-doesn't grin.

"Well…that is…it won't be too cold for me," I tease. "But if Marcy falls in the ditch again—she could have a cold butt." I can't help but chuckle when I think of the look on Marcy's face when she slid in the ditch.

"Yeah, yeah, yeah," Marcy says. "I'll probably never hear the end of it."

"Nope!—You won't." I say and chuckle some more.

"It is kind of funny," Martha says and chuckles too. She pulls the car over to the side of the road in front of my house to let Marcy and I out.

"I see your Mother didn't hire anyone to keep the driveway plowed while she's gone," she says.

"No," I say. "She wouldn't have thought to make it easy for me." Marcy and I plow through foot high snow to the porch.

Marcy reaches for the snow shovel leaning against the house and starts pushing snow off the porch and steps.

I stomp the snow off my feet while I pull off my gloves and fumble through my pocket for the house key. We brush off our pant legs and step inside.

"It sure feels different in here since dad's been gone, doesn't it?" I say to Marcy. "—Like an empty old house."

"It does," Marcy says quietly. "And sad."

We kick our boots off and hang up our coats.

"This is where the paint is." I open the big closet door and we scan the sides of the cans to see if there is something we can use.

"Here's some white ceiling paint," I say. I try to slide the can out without disturbing the others, but it doesn't work and several cans come tumbling out.

"Good thing no covers flew off," Marcy says, laughing as she trys to stop them from rolling all over.

"Well, at least we can see them now." I laugh and sit down on the floor.

"Look at this one," I say, reaching over to grab a can with emerld green paint slopped on the side of it. "This is the color of dad's office—I like it."

"It's way too dark for a sewing room," Marcy says, "But we could mix it with some white and lighten it—that might be pretty."

"My dad said it was okay to mix paint if it is the same kind. Let's look through the rest."

We take all the paint cans out of the closet and find another can of partially full ceiling paint.

"Here's one that's called, 'Mellow Yellow' and it feels pretty full," Marcy says, shaking the can. "Do you think there would be enough in here?" She hands me the can.

"I don't know. Let's open it and see." I pick it up and take it in the kitchen. "Bring in the ceiling paint and we'll open them too," I say to Marcy.

I get a table knife out of the drawer and pop the lids off the cans.

"This ceiling paint looks okay," I say. "Do you like this yellow?"

"It's pretty—Mom would like it. Is there enough?"

"I don't know, but it's a nice light color and if we don't have enough, we can paint the wall with the shelves white. If we're going to stack your Mom's fabric on them, the fabric would look nice against the white."

"Oh, it would. I saw a can of off-white wall paint in there some where. I'll go find it."

While Marcy searches for the paint, I pound the covers back on the cans. Marcy returns with the off-white paint and we open it and find it almost half full. We stack the rest of the cans back in the closet and sort through the old paint brushes and rollers and make a pile of things to take back to Marcy's.

"We're going to have to make at least two trips to carry this back to the house," I say, dreading the thought of lugging it all.

"Unless…Marcy says. "We put it all in a clothes basket and cover it up with a couple of your shirts. I can call Mom to come pick us up and she'll think you're bringing home a basket of clothes."

"Good thinking," I say. "There should be a clothes basket on top of the dryer. You get that while I to go find my dad's Bible. I hope Mother didn't throw it out."

I climb the stairs and walk by my bedroom to dad's office. It looks so bleak with all the empty shelves. I sit down in his chair and slide up to the desk and stare at the picture of me sitting on his lap with a crooked birthday hat perched on my head. I was five years old when it was taken. My dad said it was a very special day and he braided my hair and tied a feather in it with a thin piece of leather cord. Then he bent over and kissed me on the top of my head and whispered in my ear. "Now you're a beautiful Ojibwa princess…little Marie." I laughed and said, "No daddy…it's Chickadee Marie, remember?" He smiled and sat me on the corner of his desk and took my picture.

I suppose Mother threw it away—I've never seen it. She had a fit when she saw my hair. "She's not a heathen Indian,"—she practically spit out the words. Then she yanked the feather out of my hair and pulled the braids apart. I remember crying because it hurt and because my dad looked so sad. Then mother took me downstairs and put the birthday hat on me.

"All packed!" Marcy says, and I practically jump out of my skin. "Sorry, I didn't mean to scare you."

"It's okay—I didn't hear you come up the stairs," I say. "I was wondering if Dad had any more photos of me stashed around here any where."

"We can look for some," Marcy says, "Just point me where to start."

"I don't know, maybe there are some in the desk. I'll look here, why don't you look through the file cabinet and see if there's a folder that might have photos in it."

I pull open the top drawer and find my dad's Bible. I take it out and push aside the pens, paperclips, and loose papers, and paw around in the back of the drawer.

"Hey Chickadee," Marcy says, "Here's a file folder with your name on it. It doesn't have any photos, but it has papers in it—want to take a look?"

"Yeah," I say, "Let me have it." I stand up and stretch across the desk.

Marcy hands me the file folder and I flip through the papers.

"It looks like mostly old doctor bills—but this looks interesting." I pick up an old envelope with my full name typed neatly in the middle of it. I pull out the piece of paper.

"This can't be right," I say sitting down. I slump back in the chair. I feel like I'm sinking into a deep hole.

"What is it?" Marcy says, "You're white as a sheet."

"Marcy, this is my birth certificate. Look at it—I can't believe what it says!

Marcy takes it from my hands and reads out loud:
Maiden Name of Mother: Marie Rainbow Bird

Name of Father: Unknown

I watch as Marcy's face changes from curious to confused to totally troubled. "I'm calling Mom, right now," she says. "Does this phone work?" She grabs up the phone and dials her mom.

I hear her talking—she sounds a long ways away. I pick up the birth certificate and stare at it.

Oh God, who is Marie Rainbow Bird?...Is she really my mother?...If she is then that means Mother isn't my mother?...And dad is *unknown*?...How can that be? And if it's true—who am I? Oh God, this makes no sense—has my whole life been a lie?

"Come on, Chickadee, let's go downstairs and wait for Mom. Maybe she knows something we don't." Marcy takes my hand and I follow her like a zombie down the stairs.

"This is insane," I say, "My parents aren't my parents? There is nothing on this paper that says I was adopted. I don't understand what this means. I never heard of a Marie Rainbow Bird...but Marie is my middle name. Why didn't anyone ever tell me about this, Marcy?"

"I don't know," Marcy says. "But Mom will help us get to the bottom of it. Don't worry—I think I hear her now."

We jump up and run out to the kitchen.

"Okay—" Martha says coming through the door, "What's so important that you had me walk through snow to get here—and you better make it quick—I'm parked in the road."

Before she can get her coat unzipped, I shove the birth certificate in front of her.

"Look what we found." I say trying to hold the paper steady for her to read.

"What on earth?" She says, taking it from me. "Where did you get this? Have your parents ever mentioned anything about this to you?"

"Not a word," I say.

"We were looking for some photos of Chickadee and came

across it," Marcy says.

"Martha, is it true—is it really my birth certificate? How could they have not told me? Was I adopted? How can dad not be my dad?—I look like him."

"I don't know all the answers, Chickadee—it is your birth certificate. Try to calm down—we'll get it figured out. I am calling your great Uncle Hawk right now to see what he knows and then I am calling your mother.

"Uncle Hawk? I don't have an Uncle Hawk?"

Martha looks at me like I lost my mind.

"You don't know your great Uncle Hawk?"

"No," I say, "I never heard of him."

Chapter Fifteen

"Here we are." Martha pulls into a long narrow driveway surrounded by trees. We curve around a corner to a small clearing where a deer statue stands with its head held high. It appears to be looking towards Uncle Hawk's log cabin nestled against the edge of the woods. Smoke curls out from the chimney and snow drifts are swirled around the sides of the cabin. Colorful bird houses line up on wooden posts along a fence to a shed. It reminds me of a Christmas card.

The cabin door opens and I notice large deer antlers mounted above the entrance. A slim man with two long grey braids hanging down the front of his shirt steps out on the small porch.

"That must be him," I say a little nervously.

"It is," Martha says, bringing the car to a stop. "He is very much like your father. I know you will like him. Now, let's go in and see what we can learn about your life."

Martha pushes me ahead as we make our way along the shoveled path.

"Welcome," he says. He has tears in his eyes as he steps in front of me and rests his hands on my shoulders. He studies my face for a minute before he wraps his arms tightly around me. "I was afraid this day might never come, Summer Rain."

It doesn't matter that he got my name wrong—the moment he hugs me I feel like I have known him forever. I hug him back.

Eventually we let go and he reaches to hug Martha. "Hello my friend. It has been a while since our paths have crossed. I am glad you called. And this must be Marcy," he says looking over her shoulder. "Can I give you a hug too?"

"Sure," Marcy says. She steps forward and Uncle Hawk smiles. "A hug is like a handshake of the heart," he says. "Now, come in...come in, and let's get acquainted."

Walking into Uncle Hawk's home is like walking back in time. The rustic log walls are rough and natural and grey with age. The livingroom and kitchen is one large room separated only by a round wooden table and four chairs. A big pot-bellied stove sits in the corner of the livingroom with wood stacked high in a crate next to it. The log walls are covered with Native American items. A large buffalo skull is mounted on one wall, with feathers and beads hanging down. Part of the skull is painted with red, yellow, and blue stripes and one eye is circled in black. It's beautiful.

I look around the rest of the room and try to take it all in. Something about the place is so inviting. Maybe it's the smell of coffee mixing with another slight smokey odor—not cigaraette smoke, but a more pleasant smell.

"Have a seat," Uncle Hawk says, pulling a chair out from the table for Martha. "Would you like some coffee?" he asks her.

"I'd love it, Hawk—and thanks for having us over on such short notice. But, like I said on the phone, Chickadee needs to know the truth about her parents—especially Jay—she loved him very much—he was a good dad to her."

"I'll do the best I can to help," Hawk says. "Now, you two young ones pull up a chair." He motions to Marcy and me.

"My, what is it that smells so good in here?" Martha asks.

"Sweet grass," he says, pulling a mug off a wood shelf jutting out between the logs above the kitchen counter. He pours a cup of coffee, hands it to Martha, and smiles, "I burn it to cleanse the mind, body, and spirit."

Marcy and I look at each other.

"You girls probably don't drink coffee—I have packets of hot chocolate. How would that be?" Uncle Hawk says.

"Okay," Marcy and I say together. We quietly high-five each other when he turns around and grabs two more mugs. He fills a tea kettle with water and sets it on the stove to heat. When he takes the milk out of the refrigerator for Martha's coffee something catches my eye.

"Oh my gosh—that's me." I point to a snapshot taped on the refrigerator door. I can hardly believe it—there I am with a big smile sitting on the corner of my dad's desk—my hair in braids and a feather attached.

"Where did you get that?" I ask.

"Your dad gave it to me when you were five. You were the spitting image of your mother when she was that age," Uncle Hawk says. He opens the packets of hot chocolate, hesitates a minute, and then dumps them into the mugs.

"I think I better start this story at the beginning," he says.

Martha, Marcy and I sit quietly and watch as he pours the hot water in the mugs and stirs the hot chocolate. I notice he limps slightly as he steps over to the table and puts the mugs in front of Marcy and me. He steps back to the counter and pours himself a cup of coffee.

"I talk the truth," he says, sitting down. He leans in close to me and puts his hand on mine. "Your birth mother is Marie Rainbow Bird. She was my niece and Jay's sister. When she was young, she went away to college and fell in love—before long she found out you were on the way. At the same time—she found out her young man was not what she had thought and they parted. Her dad—your grandpa—and I couldn't talk her into coming home. She insisted she could keep her job, continue school part-time, and raise you—so Jay was determined to help her. He and Robin had been married only a short time when this all came about. They were living down near

Madison then and were fairly close to where Marie was living." He stops and takes a sip of coffee.

"Well, a few weeks before you were born, Marie started having woman problems and the doctor put her in the hospital to keep track of her—but in the end—she went the way of her ancesters. She died the day you were born. Jay was devastated. He and Marie were always close. There was a time I didn't think he would get over it." He stops and takes another sip of coffee.

"Then all of a sudden Jay appeared to be better. I asked him what turned things around and he told me he found Jesus and that made all the difference in the world to him."

I can see Uncle Hawk still has tears in his eyes, but he doesn't try to hide them.

I put my other hand over his and squeeze. He smiles at me.

"Well, there is something else I gotta tell you—young one. I don't want to hurt your feelings, but you might as well know all the truth." He pauses for a minute and looks at me like he's trying to decide if I will understand what he's about to say. "I don't know how you feel about Robin taking over as your mother, but I have tell you straight out—I don't have much use for that woman."

"I don't either," Martha says before I can answer. "Robin doesn't have a compassionate bone in her body! I'm going to call and talk to her about this, but I want to get all the facts straight first. Now, did Jay and Robin legally adopt Chickadee?"

"I don't think so," Uncle Hawk says. "Robin was of a mind not to have any young ones. Jay told me he hadn't realized that when they got married and it was a sore spot between them. He said he had a lot of talking to do to get her to agree to help raise this young one. He finally told her she didn't have a choice if she wanted to stay married to him."

"Anyway," he says to me, "Summer Rain, there was no way your daddy was going to let anyone raise his sister's child, but him. He went and saw a lawyer and signed some kind of legal papers, but I don't believe you were ever officially adopted."

I can't keep letting him call me by the wrong name so I say: "Didn't my dad tell you my name is Chickadee?"

Uncle Hawk raises his eye brows.

"Oh he told me," he says, shaking his head. "But Marie called you Summer Rain and that is what you will always be to me. Marie came to visit when she was full of child. She sat right there on that couch rubbing her belly and talking about how happy she was going to be when you were born. She told me she knew you were a girl and would call you Summer Rain. I asked her how she came up with that name. She said, 'When the Great Creator sends the warm summer rain, it cleans Mother Earth and gives her a fresh new beginning.' She told me you were going to be born in the summer and that is how she thought of you—as bringing her a fresh new beginning."

"Jay—your dad knew that," he continues. "But Robin—she has some sort of resentment against Indians. I guess she never figured out Jay was part Ojibwa until after they were married." He let out some kind of snort and chuckles.

"Anyway, Jay told me they got in an argument over naming you Summer Rain, because she—'wasn't going to raise no Indian.' He said when they were arguing a chickadee landed on the windowsill and so he said why don't they name you Chickadee. He reasoned that if her name was Robin Bird and his was Jay Bird it would be okay if you were a Chickadee Bird. Robin finally gave in. But, like I said, you will always be Summer Rain to me."

All the Christmas Eve's I can remember flash through my mind. I see my Dad—every year—handing the chickadee ornaments to me one at a time to hang on the tree. All the while he would tell me the story of how I was named Chickadee. It made me feel so special and I had believed every word. How many half-truths have I been told all my life? I take a deep breath—I don't want to cry. It seems as though all I have done for a year is cry. Help me God to be strong. I want to know the rest of the truth right now.

"So if Jay wasn't my dad—but was my uncle—who is my real dad?" I say, swallowing hard.

"He was your real dad!" Martha and Uncle Hawk both say at once. The way they smile at each other across the table, I half expect them to high-five each other.

"I know—and he was the best dad ever," I say, "But someone is my biological father. Do you know who he is?"

"Marie would never say, but before she became pregnant, she use to talk about someone named Tom. I never did hear a last name—Jay never tried to find out. He said after the way he treated Marie, he didn't want him around you. He said he would let the Great Creator take care of him. He was right—we will all stand before the Great Creator some day and account for our actions."

Just the way Uncle Hawk talks, I can tell how much he cares about me. I feel cheated out of not meeting him before now.

"I wish I could have come to visit you," I say.

"I wish you could have come too. Jay came every Wednesday night. He talked about you all the time. There isn't much about your life that I don't—."

"What…?" I say. "Wednesday night is when he stopped after work at the firehouse for a meeting with the other volunteer firemen. He said he stayed after the meeting to play cards with some of them."

"Well, he might have made an appearance at the firehouse, but he came and ate dinner with me every Wednesday night. He couldn't bring you with him because of Robin. He never told her he came here."

My mouth drops open. I can hardly believe what I am hearing. This is just too much. My eyes flood with tears and I know there is no way I am going to be able to hold them back.

"One lie leads to another," I say, choking up. "That's what dad—

I mean Jay—use to tell me—well, I guess he would know!" Tears stream down my cheeks. "How could he have kept all this from me?"

"Oh, Chickadee," Marcy says, "I'm so sorry."

"I'm sorry too, young one," Uncle Hawk says, patting my hand. "This is a lot to take in, but once you get it all sorted out in your mind, you will come to understand Jay and Robin—and even yourself—a little better."

Martha digs through her pocketbook and pulls out a handful of tissues.

"Here," she says, handing them to me. "Hawk, thank you so much for helping us clear things up. I need to take Chickadee home now. She needs some quiet time to think and absorb all this information. In time, I'm sure she'll want to come visit you again."

"How about Wednesday night—for supper?" I say, wiping away my tears. "I think I have missed enough time not getting to know Uncle Hawk."

"Why…I would like that very much," Uncle Hawk says, looking pleased. "Martha if you can drop her off, I'll see to it she gets home."

Chapter Sixteen

Dear God, it's the middle of the night and all I have done is toss and turn. I think about everything that has ever been told to me and wonder what is true and what is a lie. Not knowing is a very strange feeling.

I can compare my whole life to the church in the woods: it's real but it's not real. I know Dad's love for me was real and Your love for me is real. That part of my life I know is true. I guess that's the most important thing to know.

I am beginning to understand how the choices we make affect others. My dad told Mother she didn't have a choice about raising me, so she had to pretend to be my mother. That hurt me because I didn't know she was pretending and I grew up sad—thinking my own mother didn't like me. They should have told me everything and they chose not to. I would have been able to understand Mother better if they had been honest.

God, I decided I am going to make a choice right now. I am going to start calling my pretend parents by their real names— Robin and Jay. It's not that I love my dad any less, it's just that I don't want any more lies in my life. It hurts too much. I'm sorry I can't say I love Robin, but you know in my heart I don't. But, I don't hate her either. I don't feel much of anything toward her. I hope that is not wrong.

I am so glad I know the truth now. When Uncle Hawk told me how happy my real mother Marie was because I was going to be born, I felt something open up inside of me. I think my heart smiled. Oh, how I wish I could have known her. I have a million questions to ask Uncle Hawk about her. Thank you God for listening. I think maybe I can get some sleep now.

I slide the journal under my pillow. I am almost asleep when the phone rings. I hear Marcy jump up in a panic at the same time I do and we race down the stairs.

"Do you realize what time it is?" I hear Martha ask as we round the door to her bedroom. "I don't care what time it is in Hawaii, it's the middle of the night here. Just a minute—."

Martha looks pretty disgusted when she puts her hand over the phone.

"It's Robin. Do you believe it—she's finally returning my call. I've left her—oh, I don't know how many messages. She wants to talk to you. Are you okay with that? Because if you're not—you don't have to talk to her."

"I'm ready," I say. The fact that she is calling in the middle of the night and upsetting Martha, makes me more determined than ever to set things straight. "It's time for the truth."

"Hello Robin," I say, watching the reaction on Marcy and Martha's face. I have to turn away so I don't laugh right in the phone.

"When did you stop calling me Mother?" Robin asks.

"When I found out you weren't." I say in the same hard tone of voice as hers.

"Listen here, Chickadee, I may not have birthed you, but I am still your mother."

"No, Robin—you aren't my mother. You never wanted to be my mother. You only pretended to be because you felt you had no choice. Well, now I know the truth, so your obligation to dad is over and you don't have to pretend any longer."

"Just because you were snooping through the house and found your birth certificate doesn't give you the right to be disrespectful to me."

"I'm sorry—I am not trying to be disrespectful, Robin, I'm being honest and I think it is time you were honest with me."

"Stop calling me Robin! I am your mother! Your father and I have raised you the best we know how. I think you have had it pretty good, young lady. You've never lacked for anything."

"Except the truth," I say.

"Put Martha on the phone right now!"

"No, I haven't said what I want to say."

"I SAID: PUT MARTHA ON THE PHONE RIGHT NOW!"

I can feel my legs start to shake, but I am not giving in—not this time—it's too important. I take a deep breath and stand up straight. Marcy and Martha are sitting on the edge of the bed. Marcy has her eyes shut and looks like she is praying. I know it must be for me.

"Be strong," Martha whispers and gives me a thumbs up.

Help me God, I pray and take another deep breath.

"I will give the phone to Martha in a minute—but first—I want to tell you I met my Uncle Hawk and know the whole truth about my real mother and father. I know that I am at least part Ojibwa Indian. And dad was too-whether you like it or not." I hear a click on the line and pause to be sure she didn't hang up on me. When I hear her breathe, I go on.

"I am not going to Hawaii and live with you and Stanley—you didn't adopt me, so you can't force me to. Uncle Hawk is my only living relative. I know he will fight for me because you have kept me from knowing my Native American heritage too long. I am going to get all my things from the house and bring them here and stay with Martha. She and Marcy love me and I am welcome here."

My knees feel like they are about to buckle. I hand the phone to Martha and run out to the livingroom and crash on the couch in tears.

Marcy comes out of the bedroom and closes the door behind her. She hands me a box of tissues and I blow my nose.

"Wow—I can't believe how brave you are," she says. "I don't know if I could have stood up to her like that."

"I didn't know if I could either—but it's the truth and I had to say it. And I wasn't brave at all—I was to scared to hear what she would say, so I gave the phone to Martha and ran. I hope Robin doesn't start yelling at her."

"Don't worry—Mom can hold her own."

"Thank you God, for Martha," I say.

"That's for sure," Marcy says, getting up. "I'm going to put on a pot of coffee for her. She is going to want some when she comes out of there."

I wipe my eyes one more time and blow my noise. I wonder how many tears a person can cry before their eyes dry up for good. I must be close to the limit by now.

Marcy comes back in and sits next to me and takes hold of my hand. We sit quietly, listening to the coffee pot gurgle. It's almost half an hour before Martha comes out of the bedroom.

"Oh, bless you my child," she says following the aroma of coffee to the kitchen.

Marcy and I follow her and sit down at the table. I study Martha's face while she fixes her coffee, but I can't tell what she's thinking.

"Well," Martha says, pulling the chair out and squeezing in between us. "That was quite a conversation. It basically boils down to this: It seems Robin doesn't mind giving up the responsibility of raising you, but her big worry is Stanley's reaction if she does. He was looking forward to having a family and he was sure he could win you over."

"Fat chance," I say.

"So Mom—tell us—is Chickadee going to be able to stay here?"

"Yes, for now. Robin has agreed to let you stay until school is out. But, she says she has to discuss with Stanley whether it can be permanent."

"It is none of Stanley's business what I do! What is wrong with her anyway? Doesn't she get it? I am not her daughter and I am never going to live with Stanley Hood!" I jump up from the table and start pacing.

"Calm down, Chickadee," Martha says. She takes hold of my hand and pulls me back to the chair. "Here—sit. Let's talk about this rationally—shall we?"

"I'll try," I say. "It just makes me so angry."

"Well," Martha says, "Think about this: We all know how unpredictable Robin can be, but there is one thing we can always count on: Robin looks out for Robin."

"That's for sure," Marcy and I both say at once. I give her a weak high-five.

"Anyway," Martha continues, "We know she would prefer to live alone with Stanley, so let's just give her a few days to work on him, okay?"

"I guess I can stand a few more days. I just wish it could be over. But I will never live with Stanley—I—I'll run away to the North Pole first!"

"Come here you silly girl." Martha pulls me over and wraps her arms around me. "Don't worry—you won't have to tough it out at the North Pole. If Robin doesn't get back to me in a few days, you can be sure I'll be calling her. She's just beginning to learn how much I'll fight for you and she certainly knows enough about your Uncle Hawk not to want to do battle with him."

"Oh my gosh," Marcy says. "I just thought of something funny." She starts to giggle.

I just look at her—I can't think of anything about this situation that is funny.

"What?" Martha says.

"Well, Robin married Stanley—right?" Marcy says, still giggling, "So what's her new name?"

Martha and I look at each other and smile.

"Robin Hood!" We both say at once. Martha laughs.

"That is pretty funny," I say and start laughing too.

"Mom, you better get bows and arrows ready if you're going to battle Robin Hood." Marcy says bursting into full laughter.

"Hawk can help in that department," Martha says, laughing louder.

Then all three of us keep laughing and cracking jokes—one after the other—until we are practically rolling on the floor.

Chapter Seventeen

"You're being awful quiet over there," Marcy says. She is at one end of the attic and I am at the other—both on our hands and knees with buckets and scrub brushes.

"Yeah—I was just thinking about dinner tonight with Uncle Hawk. " I drop the brush in the pail of now muddy water and sit back on my knees. "Hey—Look how shinny the floor is when it dries."

"It looks great," Marcy says. "But I wish we were done—it's hard work. When we get through, let's take the rest of the day off."

"Okay," I say. "Why don't we go snowmobiling. We've been couped up inside too long. Tomorrow we can start painting. By the way, I have to hand it to you, Marcy, you sure are a good negotiater. You talked Martha into getting rid of almost everything up here."

"Yeah, I did good," she says grinning ear to ear.

"You know," I say, " We will need help moving some of the bigger things up here—like the cutting table. I know we're not suppose to have company when Martha's not home, but do you think it would be okay if I ask Uncle Hawk to help us?"

"Well," Marcy says, "I suppose it would okay. It is for a special reason and he is an adult—and Mom does like him. I saw how they they kept looking at each other when we were at his cabin. There were sparks flying between them."

"Really? I didn't notice. I was pretty upset at the time. Oh—but, come to think about it, I did see them smile at each other when they said the same thing at the same time. I thought for a minute they were going to high-five each other across the table like we do."

"Wouldn't it be too cool if they fell in love?" Marcy says, sounding all dreamy. "I don't think Mom has dated any one since I was born. She should have somebody to love—don't you think—I mean besides us—of course."

"You don't think he's too old for her?" I ask.

"Well, he can't be that much older, Chickadee. And so what if he is—Mom likes him a lot—I can tell."

"Why don't we invite him to her birthday dinner and see what happens?"

"Oh yes—let's do," Marcy says, her face beaming. "We won't tell her—we'll surprise her!"

"Okay," I say, "But let's get this done so we can get outside."

We turn back to scrubbing the floor. We manage to finish before noon and settle in the kitchen for an early lunch.

"Do you want to ride up to Cemetery Ridge and look around?" Marcy asks.

"You know I do."

"Okay," Marcy says. "I'll call Mom." Marcy hops up to get the phone.

I clean the table off and put the dishes in the dishwasher. It will be nice to get outside and move around in the fresh air.

"Mom says it's fine as long as she knows where we're going and we're not to decide to take off some where else—and we're to call when we get back. She also said while we are all bundled up to stack some more firewood on the back porch and bring in a couple of armloads for the fireplace. And then she added it would be nice if we had time to pick up around the house a bit and run the vacuum cleaner. Other than that—" Marcy chuckles, "It's fine if we go."

"Okay," I say, "I'll stack the wood if you run the vacuum cleaner."

"Deal—let's do it when we get back," Marcy says dragging her snowmobile suit out of the closet and stuffing herself in it.

I bundle up in my coat and tuck my hair under my hood. Five minutes later, I'm riding on the back of Marcy's snowmobile and we're heading to the house to pick up mine.

The first thing I do when we get there is check the gas tank on my snowmobile.

"Wow," I say, "Harold filled it up. That was nice of him."

"Good—go get your snowmobile suit on and let's go," Marcy says.

I trot up to the house and while I'm putting on my snowmobile suit, I decide it's a good time to make a quick trip through the house and check on everything so I won't have to come back for a while.

"Okay," I say, flying out the door, "I'm ready—let's do it."

We start our snowmobiles and fly across the meadow. Marcy follows and we wind our way through the woods to the old trail road along Cemetery Ridge to the abandoned cemetery. I pull up in front of the crooked headstones sticking through the snow. Marcy pulls up beside me and we shut off our engines.

"This is where I found the path to the back of the cemetery," I say.

I have to admit seeing the undisturbed snow and not a shoveled path was a little disappointing. I look beyond the few rows of headstones to where I half expected to find the cobblestone church—but of course, it's not there. All I see are trees and through their bare branches, a small meadow.

"Let's walk back there," Marcy says. "Maybe there is some piece of old foundation sticking up through the snow."

We leave our helmets on the snowmobile seats and trek through the snow.

"Look at the dates on these headstones," Marcy says. "This is an old cemetery."

"It sure is. Look at this one." I walk over to a tall pointed monument and brush snow away from the base of it so I can read all of what it says.

John Welland
1809-1879
Beloved Husband and Father
Annabelle Welland
1819-1891
Beloved Wife and Mother

I will both lay me down
in peace, and sleep:
for thou, Lord, only makest
me dwell in safety.
Psalm 4:8

"I wonder why they don't put Bible verses on headstones any more." Marcy says. "I think it's nice."

"Maybe they do—I don't know—but I think my dad—I mean Jay—would have liked one on his," I say, walking around the monument. "These smaller ones next to it have the same last name—they must be family members."

"It's funny how—as many times as we've snowmobiled or hiked by here—we never stopped to take the time to really look at these headstones before," Marcy says. "Reading them makes you realize these were real people who had real lives.

"They sure were," I say. "And they all lived their lives right in the same area as we do. Probably every one of them walked around this cemetery at one time or another—just like we are."

"It makes me wish it was taken care of," Marcy says.

"Me too," I say, brushing snow away from another headstone. "Look at this Bible verse, Marcy."

*Therefore came I forth
to meet thee,
diligently
to seek thy face, and
I have found thee.
Proverbs 7:15*

"That's nice—I like it," Marcy says, looking up. "Isn't it odd how those headstones are over there by themselves." She points to the edge of the cemetery beyond a row of trees. Four small headstones stick out of the snow facing in a different direction.

"It is odd—they seem separated from the rest of the cemetery. Let's go see what they say."

We make our way over to them.

"Oh my gosh, Marcy—look at this." I squat down and brush the snow back from the first headstone. "He was real," I whisper, dropping down on my knees. I pull off my glove and slowly trace my fingers over the worn letters.

Preacher Joe

—

*1832-1898
—Freed Slave—
A Godly Man*

Chapter Eighteen

Dear God, What an amazing day this has been. Thank You so much for directing my steps to Preacher Joe's grave. I got goosebumps when I saw his name on the headstone.

And thanks for the great supper with Uncle Hawk. It was delicious—we had venison stew and Indian fry bread. I was a little nervous about the stew. But, it turns out that I like venison after all. Uncle Hawk says it all has to do with how you take care of the meat—from the moment you shoot the deer until you set it on the table—it all has to be treated proper.

Uncle Hawk said grace. It was different from what I am used to, but it was very special. I like the way he thanked You for Mother Earth and for all the plants and animals that live to nourish our bodies. And I liked the way he asked You to help us all learn to treat Mother Earth with respect so she can continue to feed us.

While we were eating, I told Uncle Hawk all about the church in the woods.

I didn't leave out one thing. He told me it was not a dream— it was a vision and a sacred gift from the Great Creator (that's what he calls You). He said some people go their whole lives without ever experiencing one and I should be very grateful to You and I told him I was. I asked him why he thought I was given the vision and he said it was because You knew I needed it. That's what Martha said too.

Then I told Uncle Hawk about finding Preacher Joe's headstone and how it didn't have a last name engraved on it. He told me slaves didn't have last names, but lots of times when they were freed, they took their owners last name as theirs. Then he told me others went their whole lives with no last name at all.

I remembered the scars on Preacher Joe's wrists and said how sad it was to think of what he might have had to suffer before he was able to make his own choices. I said it makes my problems look pretty small.

Uncle Hawk said, "Always remember: If you're suffering— look around— you will always find someone who is suffering more—and even though that doesn't stop your suffering—it changes your thinking because that's when you realize how much you have to be thankful for." I think Uncle Hawk is a very smart man. I am so glad that he knows You and loves you too.

Uncle Hawk gave me some tobacco to sprinkle around Preacher Joe's headstone and on the ground where I saw the church. He said to say a prayer of thanksgiving when I do because it is a way of honoring Preacher Joe and showing gratitude to You. He said its similiar to folks putting flowers on a person's grave.

As soon as I got home, Martha asked me all kinds of questions about Uncle Hawk. I think Marcy is right—she likes him. She even said we should have him come here for dinner some time if he's going to be feeding me every week. I almost let it slip about her birthday dinner surprise, but Marcy gave me the look and I caught myself in time.

Martha said she was surprised we found Preacher Joe's headstone. She said the historian could find nothing about a church ever being on Cemetery Ridge. I told Martha it didn't really matter because I know what You showed me.

She and Marcy were about to sit down for a game of scrabble when I got home. They asked me if I wanted to join them, but they wouldn't let me use an open dictionary, so I passed. Spelling is not my thing. I crocheted on my scarf while they played and we chatted.

Whew, I have been writing and writing. It has been a long day and I am tired but before I say goodnight God, I want to tell You I was thinking about what Uncle Hawk said about suffering and I couldn't help but wonder: If everyone in the world who suffers stands next to someone who suffers more—at the end of the line—who would be the one to suffer the most? I think the answer must be Jesus because He loves us so much that He takes all our suffering and makes it His. No one could love us more than that!

Chapter Nineteen

"That's it—we're done with the fabric." Marcy finishes folding the last piece of printed blue fabric and places it neatly on top of the stack on the shelf. "What time is it?"

"It's almost three o'clock so we have two and half hours before Martha gets home, but don't forget Uncle Hawk is coming early."

"Right," Marcy says. "I sure hope the paint dries on the door by the time Mom gets home."

"It should," I say. Marcy and I stayed up late last night cutting out letter stencils so we could paint "MARTHA'S SEWING PALACE" on the attic door first thing this morning. We painted the letters with the emerald green paint I found at the house. The first letter was a little crooked so we decided to make them all crooked and it turned out nice. Then Marcy drew some flowers around it with some colored markers and it made a pretty border.

"We still need to frost the cake and decorate it, set the table, make the salad and pop the rolls in the oven. I am so glad Uncle Hawk offered to bring a pot of his venison stew tonight," I say.

"Me too," Marcy says. He's been so nice—we wouldn't have been able to get everything carried up here without him."

"Yeah—and he didn't hesitate when I asked him to help. I can't wait to see him and Martha together again. This time I'll be looking for those sparks you were talking about."

"I'll bet we see them, too." Marcy beams from ear to ear.

"So," she says, "Shall we finish the cake? It should be cooled by now."

"Why don't you frost the cake while I get cleaned up?" I ask.

"Okay, and I'll clean up while you make the tossed salad—then we can decorate the cake together," she says.

"Deal," we both say and high-five each other.

I run into Marcy's room and rumble through the closet for a clean shirt. I can't find anything of mine that I want to wear, so I grab Marcy's snowman sweater and head to the bathroom. By the time I finish getting ready, Marcy's already upstairs.

"Nice sweater," she says when she sees me. "I use to have one just like it."

"Well, then—you have good taste," I say. "See you in a bit." I run down the stairs to the kitchen, chuckling all the way. Whenever Marcy and I wear each others clothes, we always try to come up with some clever comment.

I pull all the salad makings out of the refrigerator and get to work—washing, slicing, and dicing.

Before long, Marcy comes cruising into the kitchen wearing my soft green velour pullover.

"Wow, I use to have a shirt just like that," I tease.

"Oh, you like it?" Marcy says, poking around the cupboard. "I went shopping on the other side of the closet and just happened across it."

"Well, it's good that you shopped today, because tomorrow part of that closet is moving across the hall to a new location," I say.

"Oh no, Chickadee," she says. "We don't have enough candles for the cake."

"Then we will have to put a "47" right in the middle of the cake with the candles we do have," I say.

She agrees and pokes the candles in the cake. Then she writes "Mom" in chocolate chips above the number and I write "Martha" in chocolate chips below it. Then we find a little container of colored sprinkles in the baking cupboard and splash them around the edge of the cake. It turns out pretty nice.

We still have about fifteen minutes before Uncle Hawk arrives, so I ask Marcy if she will braid my hair. Just as she finishes we hear a knock on the door.

"Hello Summer Rain," Uncle Hawk says and it makes me smile. He carries in a big pot and sets it on the stove and turns the burner on low.

"Yum—that smells great—I'm hungry," I say reaching for his coat. He comes over and gives me a big hug.

"Me too," Marcy says, stepping forward for her hug.

"Did you girls get everything done you wanted to? Do you need me to help you with anything?" Uncle Hawk says.

"Nope—we're ready," Marcy says, "I just popped the rolls in the oven and when Mom turns in the driveway I'll turn on the coffee. Why don't you have a seat at the table?"

"Yes, Uncle Hawk," I say pulling out a chair. "Sit over here."

"Martha is going to be mighty proud of you young ones," Uncle Hawk says. He sits down at the table. "Now which one of these places is set for Martha?"

"Right here," I say, motioning to her seat.

He takes a small bundle of red fabric tied with a string out of his shirt pocket and sets it on the table next to her plate.

"Wait until you see Martha's sewing room finished," I say. "It's beautiful. And Marcy had this great idea to sort by color that big box of buttons you carried upstairs and store them in the canning jars. We put them on the shelves by the fabric. And we put her yarn in the baby crib and oh—everything looks so pretty and colorful."

"And wait until you see how shinny we got the floor, it—," Marcy stops mid-sentence. "Did I hear a car?"

I jump up and look out the window with her.

"It's Mom—she's early," Marcy says and flips on the coffee maker.

Marcy and I stand at the door waiting. We bombard Martha with hugs and kisses when she steps in the house. She starts laughing and we sing "Happy Birthday" while we pull her coat off her and I hang it up.

"Hello Hawk—I wondered whose car was parked out there," she says still laughing. "Welcome to my crazy household." She looks over at the decorations on the table and sees the extra plate. "And welcome to my birthday dinner."

"Well, happy birthday—it's an honor to be here," Uncle Hawk says and walks over to give her a hug.

"Dinner is almost ready," Marcy says pulling the rolls out of the oven.

"First things first," Martha says. "I want to see my birthday present. You girls have been running up and down those stairs for almost two weeks now and I haven't been able to get a peek. I want to see what a clean attic looks like."

"Okay," Marcy says, trying to be nonchalant, "But—it's just an attic."

"Yeah," I say, following Marcy's lead, "We did the best we could, Martha, I hope you're not too disappointed."

"You don't mind, do you Hawk—if we all go take a quick look?" Martha asks.

"Oh no," he says. "Lead the way."

We follow Martha up the stairs to the attic door. She stops to read the sign.

"MARTHA'S SEWING PALACE?—What's this all about?"

Marcy and I shrug and walk past her up the stairs. I flip the light on and we step back and watch Martha's face as she reaches the top of the stairs. Uncle Hawk stands next to us and we all start laughing.

"Oh, my goodness—what have you done? This is wonderful! Where did you get the paint? How did you get everything up here? Oh, my goodness—you sorted all my fabric and stacked it so nice. Oh, my goodness—there's all my yarn—what a great way to use the crib. How did you manage to have new flooring put down? Oh, my goodness—and look at my buttons. Oh, my goodness—and my trunk, I've never seen it so clean—and I love the dolls perched on it. Oh, my goodness—Oh, my goodness—"

Marcy and I and Uncle Hawk laugh and laugh as we watch Martha wander in a circle around and around looking and touching everything and saying "Oh, my goodness," over and over until she suddenly stops in the middle of the room and starts crying. We all rush over to her and Uncle Hawk hands her his handkerchief.

"Don't cry, Mom," Marcy says.

"I just never expected anything like this. It is the most wonderful present ever given to me," she says. "How did you two manage it all?"

"Well, we got the paint from Chickadee's house." Marcy says.

"Dad has several cans stored in the backroom," I say. "And Uncle Hawk came over and helped us move the heavy stuff up here."

"Yeah, and the floor is not new—we just scrubbed it." Marcy adds.

"I am overwhelmed," Martha says. "It's so perfect—I've always wanted a room like this." She dabs at her eyes and gives us both bear hugs. "I love you girls so much."

"They sure did a great job turning your attic into a sewing palace," Uncle Hawk says with a smile. "Now, if you would like, Martha, I can come over and take down that bare light bulb and put up some track lighting for you."

"Oh, Hawk—how nice of you. That would be wonderful." Martha says.

"Are you ready for some birthday dinner now?" I ask, hearing my stomach growl.

"I certainly am," Martha says, "It's time for us to sit, relax, eat and chat. But, I may have to run back up here a couple of times during dinner to be sure I didn't imagine all this."

Chapter Twenty

Dear God, It's Martha's birthday and I feel like it's mine.
Tonight was so special. When Marcy and I saw Martha's face
when she looked around her new sewing room, it made all the
hard work worth it. She was so happy.
·And, Marcy is right. Martha and Uncle Hawk do have sparks
flying between them. When Martha opened the little bundle
Uncle Hawk put by her plate, I could tell she really likes him
because her face got kind of flushed—like when I talk to Harold.
Uncle Hawk made her a necklace out of different colored beads
and it had a tiny carved red-tailed hawk in the middle of it.
Martha put it right on. I bet she doesn't ever take it off.
But God, the most wonderful thing of all happened. After
dinner when we were all sitting around the fireplace chatting,
Martha announced she had had another great birthday present
today.
She said Robin called her at work and they had a long talk.
Robin and Stanley came to an agreement when Robin told him
I wasn't her real daughter. They agreed Martha could file to be
a legal guardian for me. But Martha said she didn't want to.
When I heard that, I thought my heart was going to stop right
then and there.
But, then Martha said, she wanted to adopt me, instead. I
jumped up and hugged her so hard. Marcy jumped up and
hugged me and said we would be sisters for real. Then Martha
and Marcy and I all cried and hugged each other. Even Uncle

Hawk had tears. I can hardly write this God, because I am crying now, but this time it is because I am so happy. I am looking forward to spending every day with my new family for the rest of my life. And I am looking forward to learning all about my Ojibwa heritage. Uncle Hawk says I will learn to build a rainbow bridge between living in the white man's world and the Ojibwa world so that I can have the best of both. I'm not exactly sure what that means, but I am ready to learn.

And another thing God, when I was digging out my pajamas tonight, I came across my dad—Jay's—old flannel shirt. I realized I haven't worn it once since I have been here. I haven't even thought about it. I hugged the shirt close to my heart because Jay was a good dad to me and I will always love him, but I guess I don't need to curl up in it and feel sorry for myself any longer. Some day I am going to ask Martha if she will help me make a pillow out of it and I will keep it forever.

And, God—You know how You have a reputation of working in strange and mysterious ways? Well, I am not fooled. I know You are behind everything that has happened to me. Some of it has been hard to understand, but now I can see how You have worked to rearrange my whole life and it couldn't be better. Thank You. Thank You. Thank You.

So now I will say good night God. I love You and I will forever keep You right in the middle of my heart.